# Dark Abandon
## by
## Kallie Lane
### Shadow Soldiers Suspense
### Book 2

**DARK ABANDON: A Shadow Soldiers Suspense Novel**

Publishing History

First edition published 2012, The Wild Rose Press, Inc.

Second edition published 2021, Kathryn Donaldson

Digital ISBN 978-0-9918138-9-6

Print ISBN 978-0-9918138-8-9

Published in the United States of America

# Dedication

This book is dedicated to the brave men and women of the Canadian military, both active and retired.

To my personal heroes, my sons, Chris and Dave. You always make me proud!

To my readers, with heartfelt thanks.

# Acknowledgements

**Very special thanks** to Coreene Callahan, Fred Donaldson, Maggie Jagger, Lesley Lawrence, and JJ Wilhelm for your wonderful insights, encouragement and friendship.

# Chapter 1

*Silver Lake*

Melena Salera downshifted on the curve of serpentine road, revving the RPMs to clear the top of the next rise. She shifted smoothly into fourth gear, after cresting the peak, and opened up the big V8 on the straightaway. The vintage '76 Firebird roared along the winding ribbon of asphalt, the upbeat tempo of *Higher Love* cranking through the speakers. Melena joined in and belted out the chorus. She tapped the rhythm on the steering wheel until a movement in her peripheral vision caught her attention. She slammed on the brakes with both feet. A deer gamboled across the highway as the Firebird screeched to a shuddering halt.

Clenching her teeth, she swallowed the lump in her throat that might have been her breakfast burrito while the deer trotted for cover on the opposite bank of road. Too late, Melena remembered those deer crossing signs she had ignored for the last several miles and breathed a huge sigh of relief. The deer had escaped unharmed. Fingers still clutching the steering wheel, she started off again, this time at a sedate pace with the radio switched off.

She wrapped her scattered thoughts around the reason for making this trip into the wilderness. Well, perhaps not quite the wilderness, but she was a city girl and anything outside the burbs was like the boondocks to her.

Her return flight to Montreal had touched down from Chicago that morning. As a sales trainer for a leading pharmaceutical company with branches in both the U.S. and Canada, Melena travelled back and forth regularly.

Based on the urgent nature of the messages left on her answering machine, she had retrieved her car from airport parking, used GPS to get directions, and, with her usual impulsiveness, sped the hundred and thirty kilometers into the Laurentian mountain region. A sign for Silver Lake glinted in the sun and she angled into the turn. It wouldn't be long now before she came face-to-face with the owner of that smooth-as-cognac voice. Although, were she honest with herself, the lawyer had sounded surly when he demanded she meet him at Silver Lake. Even so, his voice had been full-bodied and rich, a voice capable of stirring any woman's fantasies.

*Oh, right, Mel. He is probably five feet tall, is bald as a billiard ball and weighs over three hundred pounds. When are you going to get it through your head? Knights in shining armor are only found in romance novels.*

By the time she pulled up to the boat docks, the road had dead-ended at the water. Where was she supposed to meet the lawyer? Noting a white-clapboard building, a general store with gas pumps and a phone booth out front, she parked her ride. A bell tinkled when she opened the door to the store.

An older man, pear-shaped, dressed in tan shorts and a T-shirt with a fishing hat perched on his head, chatted with the reed-thin woman behind the counter. Melena nodded at them then headed for the row of fridges at the back of the store. Her sandals scraped the linoleum as their voices followed her up the narrow aisle.

"Doc, is there any news yet on the funeral service for Sarah Davidson?"

"Nothing yet, Stella. Theo hasn't had a chance to iron out the details. He charged out of here a few days ago to deal with an emergency in Mallard Bay. He should be back tomorrow at the latest."

"I hope so. The women's auxiliary needs to prepare the food and set everything up for the luncheon," Stella grumbled.

Melena processed that bit of news. *Theo? Could he be the lawyer, Theo Sauvage, who contacted me?* She had raced here to meet him and he wasn't even available.

Doc's voice continued as she stopped at a rack loaded with chips to the left of the cash register, pretending to look while she eavesdropped. "Theo told me he needs to speak with a friend of Sarah's, a man named Mel Salera before he can arrange for her burial."

Melena swallowed a gasp. She didn't know anyone named Sarah. *Why would the lawyer need to contact me about the woman's funeral arrangements? And why does he think I'm a man?*

"I don't know anything more than that." Doc rubbed his chin as though deep in thought. He pushed back the brim of his fishing hat to run a hand over his thinning hair. "Either way, the funeral will be held in the next few days. Theo is not going to drag it out longer than necessary. He loved Sarah like a grandmother."

"We all loved her, Doc," Stella said, a sad note in her voice. "It's hard to believe she's gone."

Her mind reeling, Melena abandoned the chips rack, paid for the soda, and left the store with the couple still deep in conversation. Her curiosity was peaked. *What's this all about?* Even if the lawyer wasn't available, she should at least talk to the locals to find out what was going on. Jogging down the stairs, she headed for the waterfront while formulating a plan.

*Oomph!* She ploughed into a wall of solid muscle. Strong fingers snaked her wrists as the man's gaze raked her body with chilling insolence, his mouth forming a sneer as he catalogued her diminutive size, spiky hair and icy stare.

He dressed to impress. Designer labels galore. Gold chains hung around his neck with enough karats to pay Melena's grocery bill for a year. His dark hair was tied at the nape with a strip of leather. Not unpleasant to look at, but repulsive all the same.

It was obvious that he liked to control. He also liked to inflict pain, judging by his grip on her wrists. *A sleaze with money.* The harder she tried to break his hold, the harder he held on. *Damn him.*

She glanced around, hoping to catch someone's attention since she couldn't reach the cell phone in her pocket. Not that calling 9-1-1 would do any good. There probably wasn't a police station for miles.

Cripes, no-one on the docks was near enough to see she was in trouble. Short of screeching her head off, she was on her own with this thug. And pride wouldn't allow her to scream. Not yet, anyway.

"You know," he challenged, pulling her harder against him, "a woman could get hurt throwing herself at the wrong man."

"Really? Not if the man in question gets slammed in his cul-de-sac," she snapped, shoving her leg between his thighs. "You have five seconds to release me before I knee your junk to hell and back. One...two...three..."

Anger flashed in his eyes. He didn't let go. She wouldn't back down, praying he wouldn't notice her trembling as she tensed her leg muscles to deliver the promised blow.

"Bitch." He released her on the count of five then cocked a thumb and index finger in her direction. "I owe you one."

"Jerk." Melena got her feet moving, skirted around him, and headed for the docks. His glare burned a hole between her shoulder blades as she hustled toward the safety of families loading provisions into their boats. She forced herself to relax and put the idiot out of her mind. By the time Doc meandered down to the lake a short time later, she had herself under control. She fell into step beside him.

"I heard you talking at the store. I'm Melena Salera, the person Theo Sauvage is trying to contact. He's obviously not here, and I don't know where to find him. Can you help me out?"

Pulling up short, Doc set down his gas can and eyeballed her with an arctic blast. *Why the chilling stare?* She struggled to hold her ground and wait him out. A moment later and his bitter expression morphed into a grin. *What in heaven's name is the matter with him?*

"Theo will be back tomorrow morning at the latest," he said. "He booked a room for you at the local B & B on the off chance you showed up. You'll be mighty comfortable there."

"I don't know..." Melena yearned to sleep in her own bed tonight. This seemed like a wild goose chase. Still, she was exhausted, too tired to move really, much less drive back to Montreal. Besides, the thought of coming all this way for nothing rankled. Her bulging shoulder bag bumped against her hip as she tugged it higher, reminding her of its contents, everything from passport, keys and wallet to a change of clothes, toothbrush and cosmetics.

She never travelled without overnight amenities in her purse when she checked her luggage on a flight. Everything she needed to spend the night was right there, so why not bunk in and wait it out? "All right, I'll stay, but I can only stay one night. If the lawyer doesn't show tomorrow, I'm headed home."

"Can't ask for more than that, little lady." Doc did a little jig, picked up the gas can again and hustled for the docks, snagging her elbow and dragging her along. "Come on. Let me gas up my boat and I'll take you to the Home Sweet Home B & B."

*Yikes! Is the man harmless or insane?*

Muttering under her breath, she asked herself, "Should I go with him?"

Fool that she was...she went.

Maybe not her smartest or smoothest move. Her nose crinkled in disgust. It was possible no one at the B & B would know anything about Theo's reason for summoning her to the lake. Still, Melena intended to investigate and see if she could discover why the lawyer had insisted on meeting her. Pumping Doc for information ended up being a colossal waste of time. His lips were sealed shut on the subject. She settled instead for the rush of wind on her face, sunshine reflecting off foam-green waves, and the vista of rustic cottages dotting the mountainous shoreline as they travelled down the lake.

According to Doc, the bed and breakfast was on a private island leading into the last bay. A half hour later, he pulled up alongside a boathouse, threw the fishing boat into neutral, and leaned over the side to grab hold of the pier. Melena jumped for the dock while he stretched a hand up to her with keys dangling from his fingers.

"What's this?" she asked, reaching for the ring full of old skeleton keys.

"The keys to the castle, my lady," he said, pushing away from shore before she could drop back onto the boat. "Follow the path through the trees and you'll come to a house. The big brass key is the one for the front door."

"Hold up a minute!" Panic set in with the realization Doc had pulled a fast one. "What happened to my reservation at the B & B? I want to go there. I'm not staying here by myself."

"Hells fire, there is no B & B. Didn't want to tell you before 'cause I knew you'd take off without talking to Theo. But, you'll be real comfortable at Sarah's house. Plus if Theo is delayed until tomorrow, I'll come back and check up on you. Meantime, quit your whining and get a move on. The fridge is full and you can make yourself at home." Doc reached down to adjust something on the boat. "Oh, before I forget, if you see Doodlebug, you be sure to feed him. He gets ornery when he's hungry. Actually, you should leave a door open for him, in case he gets the urge to come on home."

"Did you say doodlebug?" Doc said nothing, staring at her as if she was whining again, and waited her out. "Okay, I'll bite. What's a doodlebug?"

"Well, now," Doc harrumphed. "Doodlebug is Sarah's lap dog. He headed into the bush the night of the *accident,* and he hasn't been seen since."

"Uh-huh." Melena glared at him then eyed the distance between the boat and the dock, wondering if she could make it. Six feet was a little too much for her to jump. The old coot knew how to throw a sucker punch. "Well, since you're stranding me here, I'll make sure I feed him...if I see him."

Melena loved animals and felt instant compassion for the poor little creature. How many nights had he been alone in the woods? Besides, he'd be welcome company for her.

"Now that everything's settled, I'll contact Theo in Mallard Bay and let him know you've arrived. He'll be right anxious to make your acquaintance."

Doc backed away and threw his boat into a forward thrust, Melena gawking as he rammed his hat down on his head, gunned the engine, and tore out of the bay. "Good luck, Mata Hari. You're going to need it."

She threw her hands up in frustration while mulling over his parting words. He obviously guessed she intended to snoop around since he'd brought her here. Why else would he refer to her as a famous female spy?

Undeterred, she hiked the path through thick forest until Sarah's house popped into view on a terraced clearing with its rough-hewn logs, natural shellac with forest-green trim and matching tin roof. Window boxes overflowed with red geraniums and white begonias. Hummingbirds flitted to bright red feeders hanging beneath the porch eaves. Melena climbed the stairs onto a wide-planked porch and inhaled a deep breath of pine fragrance.

Her conscience prickled for a few seconds. Her self-appointed role of investigator weighed her down. Her actions were an invasion of the dead woman's privacy. Still, she'd been dumped here by Doc and had nowhere else to go. She might as well do what she came to do.

The key turned smoothly in its lock. Remembering the missing dog, Melena braced the door open with her handbag before she entered the house. A sigh of pleasure escaped as she took in her surroundings. Sunlight streaming through skylights reflected burnished log walls and gleaming hardwood floors. Floor-to-ceiling windows stood on either side of a massive fieldstone fireplace, a flock of intricately carved geese poised to take flight from its mantle.

Overstuffed furnishings in bold primary colors scattered the living space. A footstool here, an occasional table there, with potted plants and trailing greenery perched on every available surface. Antique bookcases, low and rambling, held everything from the classics to contemporary suspense and historical romance novels.

The smell pervading the cabin was a pleasant blend of wood smoke, scented lamp oil, and lemon polish. A screened sundeck opened the far side of the room to rattan furniture and the outdoors. She loved the house. An oasis in a hectic world, and she suspected it reflected Sarah Davidson's easy-going lifestyle.

Melena's sense of right and wrong nudged her again for invading the dead woman's space. Her throat tightened with guilt. She sauntered to the kitchen and the fridge, hoping to find a bottle of wine to drown her scruples. No such luck. Bottled water would have to do.

*Drink your water, Mel, then go find something interesting to read, and mind your own business. The lawyer will be here soon enough to toss you out on your keister.*

A growl came from somewhere behind her. She froze then turned slowly toward the sound. One quick look and her legs almost folded. The largest wolf she had ever seen slinked toward her from the same doorway she had walked through a minute ago. He stared at her through flame-gold eyes, his gaze never leaving her face.

Melena had no doubt—Doodlebug had come home to roost. Except, he wasn't a pint-sized lap dog, and he wasn't happy to find a stranger in his dead mistress's kitchen. The wolf's head lowered as his ears flattened. His lips curled back to expose sharp, fanged teeth. A desperate glance told her she would never make it to the door before the animal tore her to pieces.

Eyes wide, her only defense was to mouth a silent prayer. The wolf's hackles rose. She stopped praying when he lunged toward her. A terrified giggle bubbled up as she realized she had been set up by a cunning old fox.

*Touché, Doc. I'm a dead woman because of you.*

An instant later, the wolf sent her crashing to the floor.

# Chapter 2

Theo Sauvage was beyond exhaustion as he guided the Bayliner over black, churning waves. The mountains on the horizon and distant lights of cottages faded into the misty night around him.

His body was bruised and battered, his mind taking side trips of its own. He looked and felt like hell. The last few days had taken their toll in more ways than one.

The killing spree and kidnapping in Mallard Bay had involved him personally; his brother's fiancée had been caught in the crosshairs of a deranged serial killer. Her safe return had required Special Ops precision rather than police procedure. Sully, a homicide lieutenant with Montreal P.D., had relied on him and other members of their reserve military unit to get the job done.

Theo had been glad to answer the call, to assist his brother every way that he could. Anything else would have been unthinkable. Yet, the bloody aftermath ate through to his soul. It always did. Commando tactics were never a best case scenario for him, even when there were no other options. He hated that the defining moments of his life centered on death and the dying, an inescapable pattern he had to lose. He needed to shut down those images and move on.

He sighed, rubbing the fatigue from his eyes. It was nothing a week of sleep wouldn't cure, except right now he had to deal with a piranha. Mel, or rather, Melena Salera.

He had been shocked to find out Salera was a woman, given the brutality of the crime he suspected her of committing. Doc had called him with the news a few hours ago, while he was celebrating the end of the psycho's reign of terror with the good citizens of Mallard Bay and getting a jumpstart on Sully's engagement announcement.

To say he was dumbstruck to learn Melena Salera had already planted herself at Sarah Davidson's country property was putting it mildly. After all, he hadn't been able to speak with a live body in the week of dumping messages into her generic voicemail. Yet, here she was, with Sarah's corpse barely cooled off at the morgue.

The autopsy results should be ready in a day or two. Then the wheels of justice would grind into high gear while he took a front row seat. After all, he was the attorney of record for Sarah's financial empire and would be kept appraised of the investigation into her death. He certainly didn't need to read the autopsy report to know foul play was involved.

The boating accident didn't wash with him. The sheer violence of it rocked him to the core. He would never believe Sarah had strayed off course and crashed into those rocks under her own steam, causing the boat explosion and her death. No, she had driven that lake at night for years. She was experienced and knew the dangers. She even knew where the rocks lurked beneath the waterline.

Hadn't she shown him enough times when he was a kid running the lake in his little tin can? Yeah, hadn't she yelled at him for standing up in the boat and for not wearing a life-vest? Hell, she had taught him everything there was to know about boating.

A starry sky with a full moon, it hadn't been foggy on the night of her death. Besides, Sarah had GPS installed on her boat and could steer her way without benefit of clear skies and mountain peaks to guide her. Had she been drugged and disoriented? Or had another boat ploughed her into the rocks? Both scenarios were plausible, and Sarah's murder had been the game plan.

His gut twisted, insisting Sarah had been slaughtered for her money. Theo had read the will. He knew Melena Salera was the sole beneficiary to Sarah's millions. It stood to reason she was also behind his friend's death. He intended to find out. He also needed proof that Melena was the Mel Salera listed as recipient in Sarah's will. Why refer to her as 'Mel' in the legal document?

He berthed the Bayliner in the boathouse, shut down the engine, and trekked the long path up to the house. The front door stood open. It was pitch dark inside the cabin. His senses on full alert, he moved with stealth through the rooms until he heard moans coming from the kitchen. Crossing over the threshold, he found Doodlebug. Crouched in the middle of the floor on top of a petite woman, his gigantic paws framing her head, the wolf was nose-to-nose with her.

"What do you have there, Dood?" Theo switched on overhead solar lighting, crouched beside the wolf and scratched between his ears. "Is that your dinner? What's the matter? You couldn't drag her over to your bowl?"

Dood moved his head in Theo's direction and whined. A pair of wide blue eyes flashed daggers at him from beneath the wolf's chin. "This *beast* has been lying on me for hours. I can't move and it's almost impossible for me to breathe. Get him off me."

No doubt irritated by her tone, the wolf turned back to its quarry and growled. Doc was right. Melena Salera was a pretty little thing, from what Theo could see through the wolf's fur. And hell, her eyes weren't just blue—they were cobalt blue. A short pixie hair cut, oval face and full lips, combined with those eyes, made her a very pretty package. *Shit.* Just what he needed. An attractive murderer. Theo stroked Doodlebug's head again.

"You know, I don't think I heard the magic word in that sentence. And I wouldn't call him a beast, if I were you. He takes offense to that kind of language."

The woman could barely get the words out through her clenched teeth. "Listen, Sparky, just get this hundred-pound flea bag off of me. *Please.*"

"Ah, *please*...that's much better. But, you've got the wolf's weight wrong. He weighs in closer to one-hundred-forty."

On Theo's hand signal, Dood sprang to his feet and moved away from the woman, flopping into a sit-stay position.

"It's about damn time." The woman dragged herself off the floor and brushed the hair off her shorts and T-shirt, before she looked him square in the eyes. She started a little, seeming to notice him for the first time. "Who are you? What are you doing here?"

"I could ask you the same questions. I'm Sarah's neighbor. I saw the lights on and stopped in to make sure no one's robbing the place. Who are you? And what are *you* doing here?"

"I'm Melena Salera, and I-I'm a friend of the family." She studied the floor, the walls, looked everywhere in the room but at him. "I c-came for her funeral."

Not a bad answer, Theo decided. But she's a terrible liar.

"What happened to your face? You're black and blue."

His fingers grazed the sutures above his left eyebrow. They were a grim reminder of his close brush with death, courtesy of the maniac who had rammed him from behind into the pole. With no airbags in the vintage 'Vette, he was lucky his larynx hadn't been crushed from impacting the steering wheel. As it was, he wouldn't be crooning in the shower anytime soon, not with the raspy sounds coming from his throat.

Theo refocused on the woman in front of him. "Let's just say I lost the fight between a telephone pole and my Corvette."

He wouldn't give her the time of day, except he had to inform her about Sarah's will. Give her the sealed envelope in his possession. He needed to know what was in that envelope, but he wouldn't lay his cards on the table yet. Nah, he'd toy with her first, before he tackled the legal aspects of her inheritance. After all, Sarah would still be alive if it wasn't for her. He was sure of it.

His gaze took her in with one glance. Perfect. She had a body made for sin. If the circumstances were different, he'd be playing her like a mandolin by now. She smelled of vanilla overlaid with a sensuous whisper of musk. A spicy, provocative scent that promised a man the moon and the stars waited for him in her arms. All he had to do was reach out.

He reined in his libido, scooped up Dood's bowl, and filled it with kibble before replenishing the water dish from bottled water in the fridge. The taps weren't working. He hadn't pumped water into the holding tank since Sarah's death.

"Did you ever stop to think you shouldn't be drinking and driving, Sparky?"

He swung around at Melena's sharp comment as she attempted to brush past him into the hallway. He shot out an arm and blocked her path.

"The name's not Sparky. And just for the record, sugar, I wasn't drinking and driving."

"I'm not your sugar. And if you weren't drunk, then you should consider driving lessons." She dodged under his arm and headed down the hallway at a half-trot. "Being a lousy driver is nothing to be ashamed of."

He waited until she closed the bathroom door before ruffling Dood's fur and giving him his next command. The wolf licked his hand as if in agreement. Satisfied, Theo strode out of the house and into the darkness. He stopped on the path and waited for the sound he knew was coming. Melena didn't disappoint him as she let out a blood-curdling scream. She had a great pair of lungs. Tossing his keys in the air and whistling, he made his way back down to the dock.

Score round one for the home team and Sarah. He'd be back early in the morning to go a second round with Ms. Salera. No way was he finished with her yet. Not by a long shot.

MELENA TOOK CARE OF business but was unable to wash her hands. There was no water coming from the taps. She opened the bathroom door, about to yell at Sarah's neighbor to turn on the water. The wolf stopped her in her tracks. His growling resumed full-scale once he saw her framed in the doorway. She let out a shriek as Dood lunged for the door opening.

Slamming the door in the nick of time, she bolted it, resigned to spending an uncomfortable night in the tub. That was some lapdog Sarah had struck up a friendship with. There was no way she would brave another confrontation. She wished she had her purse with at least a change of clothes and her toothbrush.

"Jerk!" Her body vibrated with anger. It was the neighbor's fault she was in this predicament. The insufferable man should have put the wolf outside. She would tell him so. Tomorrow. Once she knew his name, of course.

She tried to settle in the tub. She grumbled, shifted a few times, and allowed her thoughts free rein. Whoever the man was, he had a lot going for him in the brawn department, even if he was an unfeeling brute. At least six-four, he was easy on the eyes once you got past the bruises. His lean body was sculpted with hard muscle. Coffee-colored eyes and sable-brown hair offset a rugged, chiseled face.

Her heartbeat thrummed as she remembered his virile scent, part soap and part clean, yummy man. Too bad about his voice though. He sounded like Louis 'Satchmo' Armstrong on a bad, bad, day. She struggled to slow her breathing after doing the physical inventory.

*Remember his asinine qualities instead, Mel.*

So, yes, his upper lip had curled when he had snarled at her, just like the wolf had done. She knew she had baited him about his driving ability, but that was a reaction to her frightening afternoon spent on the floor. And maybe the fact she had no business being at Sarah's in the first place. Still, the best defense was always a strong offense, wasn't it?

Melena could hear snuffling sounds at the bathroom door. Stuffing a towel under her head, she covered her ears to block out the wolf's heavy breathing and dozed off with thoughts of the neighbor still circling her brain.

HER WATCH CONFIRMED it was barely six a.m. when the birds chirped her awake. The forest resonated with twittering and the louder sounds of animals moving through the brush. Her bones ached from sleeping in the claw-footed tub, her muscles complaining as she righted herself. What she needed was a long soak in a hot shower. Without water, that would be impossible. A dip in the lake would be the next best choice.

Gazing out the window, she judged the fall to the ground doable. She removed the screen without any trouble, hopped down to the soft earth, and slid the screen back in place. Just to be on the safe side, she tiptoed around to the front of the cabin. Yes, the front door was closed. She could have an uninterrupted swim with the big wolf still locked indoors.

It didn't take long for her to find a path down to the swimming dock. Without a swimsuit, her tangerine thong and bra would have to do. The water was refreshing and cool as she waded in and set out across the bay with sure strokes, the rising sun a warm caress on her back. After several minutes, she flipped and drifted in the slow-moving current. It felt wonderful to ease out the kinks in her spine, to float in her own world. Beneath azure skies with the occasional gull swooping overhead, the gentle pulse of waves soon lulled her into total relaxation.

She jolted to the sound of a boat closing on her. It roared at her full tilt before she could get out of its path. Waves rolled over her and she came up sputtering. Rough hands reached out and pinned her wrists, jerking her to the side of the boat.

"Well, looky here. Looks like we've caught ourselves a mermaid, boys."

The man's touch was cruel, the same man who had accosted her yesterday at the store. The expression in his eyes was feral, turning her blood to ice. He was here to get even.

Two other guys were on the boat with him, moving to the side now to reach for her legs. She managed to get her feet against the aluminum hull, pushing off with all her strength. The man's grip broke on her slippery wrists. She writhed free, diving beneath the bow to come up several feet away.

She swam for shore for all she was worth, their jeers echoing in her ears. If she could make it back to the cottage and to Dood, she would be safe. She would rather be inside with the wolf than outside with these animals.

"Yeah, you go, baby. That's right, tire yourself out. We're coming to get you."

The boat engine roared to life behind her. Within seconds, the craft moved alongside her again. Frantic now, she reversed direction and struck out toward the opposite shore. She might not make it to safety, but she would rather die trying than be caught.

The bow swung about and edged closer to her with every shuddering beat of her heart. Her breath panted out in choked sobs. Limbs cramped and threatened to seize with exhaustion. Still, she refused to give up. A hand clutched the back of her head and forced her underwater. Too late, she coiled in a dive to escape its grasp. Fingers tore at her hair and held fast.

Water seeped into her lungs. Oxygen leaked out. Despair mingled with euphoria and the realization she was going to die. Right here, right now. *No!*

The thug eased his grip and she broke the surface. Melena sucked in breaths. Then her head banged against the side of the boat. She saw stars and fought nausea. Her shoulder almost twisted from its socket when the beast wrenched her upward, out of the water.

Soon a second man clamped her waist with hands the size of ham hocks, while the third guy grappled with her ankles. Coughing and choking, blood dripped into her eyes from the gash on her forehead. Ignoring the injury, she fought like a wildcat. The thought of being raped or murdered by these pigs shot adrenaline through her muscles. She struggled harder, kicking and clawing. *I have to survive.*

"Campo, we've got company. He's coming in fast."

"What?" The ringleader's head shot up. "Hell, his boat can outrun ours. Toss her back in the drink."

Melena hit the lake with a sobbing curse and a *thank you, God* on her lips. But, Campo wasn't finished with her yet. He reached over the side, ripped off her bra and seized her throat with bruising fingers. She swiped at him with shaking fists. He shook her by the neck until she sobbed. She felt naked and ashamed, hating to show weakness to these cowards. His cold-blooded stare drilled her breasts, humiliating her while he squeezed and brutalized her flesh.

"Until the next time, bitch. And there will be a next time. You can count on it."

# Chapter 3

Theo bore down on them full throttle. Melena was back in the water, but one of the men still had his hands on her. He watched in disbelief as the man pulled back his fist and clipped her on the jaw. She sank like a rock. *Son-of-a-bitch.*

Her attackers gunned their boat and tore over the waves, lengthening the distance from his Bayliner. He didn't spare them a glance, his gaze never wavering from the spot where he'd seen her go under. He pulled in close, cut the engine and was over the side within a second.

A half hour later, he had Melena tucked in bed at the house. Doc had seen the attack on her from his dock and rushed across the bay to help.

"Jeez, Theo, who were they?" Doc Finley straightened, after covering Melena with a quilt, and turned away from the bed. "They really did a number on her."

"I don't know. When I first saw them go after her through the binoculars, I thought they were day-trippers; had hauled their boat in on the back of a trailer and slipped it in the water after dark last night. I figured they'd pulled an all-nighter, were drunk and making nuisances of themselves. But they deliberately hurt her, Doc. I think they knew her."

"Cripes, first Sarah and now this. Any chance we can find them?"

"You're kidding, right? You know what it's like. There are so many logging roads connected to the lake. These guys can just pull up on shore and stash the boat in the woods, if they haven't done it already.

Over forty kilometers of shoreline, much of it desolate, and we're talking about a small fishing boat with only a 25 HP motor."

"Like looking for a needle in a haystack." Doc repacked his medical bag and headed out the bedroom door. "I'm worried, Theo. What in blazes is happening to our peaceful little community?"

"That's what I'm going to find out." Theo raked a hand through his hair and followed Doc as far as the living room. "Is she going to be all right?"

"Her lungs are clear and nothing seems to be broken, but she needs rest. She was shaking so badly, I was more worried about her going into shock. Boy, she's a spitfire. Although, I guess I can't blame her for trying to deck me, after what she's been through. Plus, I did set her up with Dood yesterday. She has no reason to trust me."

Doc grasped his hand in a solid grip before heading outside. "Thanks for holding her down, so I could sedate her before stitching her head. She should sleep for a few hours, at least. Call me if you need me again when she wakes up. I'll keep my cell phone handy."

After Doc left, Theo walked as far as Sarah's bar and poured himself a stiff drink. It was barely eight a.m. He wasn't a morning drinker, but he needed something. He continued out to the deck and sank into the nearest chair. Tossing back the bourbon with one gulp, he glanced down at his trembling hands and shook his head.

*Oh, yeah, nerves-of-steel, Theo Sauvage, quivering like a sissy, for Pete's sake.*

Sully would get a real laugh out of this. In all their years in Special Ops, he had never experienced the knee-jerk reaction he had felt today. Melena had scared him to death when he pulled her out of the water. She hadn't been breathing. He had resuscitated her in what almost amounted to a sexual experience for him. That soft, sweet mouth fitted perfectly beneath his, her breasts molded to his chest. He was disgusted with himself for thinking that way.

Hell, she'd been terrified. She had regained consciousness in such a panic he had to hold her against him until she calmed down enough to listen to reason. His betraying body had loved every damn minute of it. What did that make him? *A perverted dirt bag, that's what.*

Sully would scoff with disgust if he could see him now. His brother had fallen for the woman he rescued from a serial killer, a wonderful woman with a dynamite kid. Meanwhile, who was he fantasizing about? Melena could be Sarah's angel of death, or worse; definitely not the kind of woman to pin his hopes on.

Seeing the bruises on her body had aroused a protective instinct in him that bordered on insane. He wanted to kill those bastards for what they had done to her. The craziest thing was he didn't even like her. He couldn't trust her. He suspected her of killing Sarah. What a freaking mess.

He heard the sound of glass breaking and hit the floor running. *What now?*

MELENA FOUGHT NAUSEA and swallowed several times. She remembered Doc giving her a shot of something, but she didn't know what. She felt so weak, her head spinning, her muscles hurting. But, God, her memory worked just fine. She had been assaulted. Now she had woken up in a strange bed. Naked.

All bad signs that pointed to one thing. She needed to get the heck out of there...to go back home where everything made sense, where she'd be safe.

A glass tumbled off the nightstand, crashing to the floor as she struggled to stand up. Her legs wouldn't hold her, as she slid off the bed.

"What are you doing?" The raspy voice shook her, although his hands were gentle as he scooped her up and laid her back against the pillows. He covered her to her shoulders again with the quilt. Sarah's neighbor...he'd saved her life this morning. "Mel, you've had an accident. Doc says you need to stay in bed a while longer to get your strength back."

"Get away from me. Don't touch me." She closed her eyes and swallowed hard. She was naked and vulnerable. The room spun and she fought to settle her stomach. But none of that mattered. She needed to get away from these people. Fast.

"My father is a very important man with the government. If you don't let me go this instant, he'll make your life a living hell."

He nodded, said nothing. Crouching by the bed, he picked up the shards of glass and stiffened. He seized her closed fist in a vise-like grip.

"Hand it over, sugar."

Melena resisted and didn't respond. She glared at him with fear churning her belly. He frightened her more than the cowards who had attacked her. He was solid, strong in mind and body. Whatever he wanted, he would take without anyone's help. Which terrified her. How the heck was she supposed to get away from a guy like him? He was too strong, too determined, too...everything!

*But he saved me...didn't he?* The details were a bit fuzzy.

Yes, he'd pulled her out of the water—and brought the doctor—so, maybe he wasn't working with the grease balls who'd hurt her. Then again, maybe he was, and this was part of an elaborate scheme to make her trust him.

Her bruised chin wobbled as he pried her fingers open to reveal the triangle of glass she had palmed only seconds before. Blood dripped from her hand and dotted the quilt.

"You've cut yourself." He reached for the first aid kit in the nightstand. "After I clean this up, I want you to sleep. You try to get out of bed again and I'll tie you to the headboard."

"Go to hell!" One look at his dark gaze told her he would make good on his threat. Panicked, she rolled for the opposite side of the bed. "You can't keep me here against my will."

Strong arms banded her in an instant, his weight covering her as he pinned her to the mattress. "Doc gave you a sedative. I can't let you loose to stumble all over the countryside. You'll hurt yourself more. Not to mention your fan club on the boat this morning is still out there. What if they come back? If they get their hands on you again, you might not be so lucky."

He smelled of sunshine and the outdoors. His breath caressed her cheek as his gaze tangled with hers. She wanted to trust him, but did she dare?

Her heart beat wildly, a bird trapped in a cage. The answering rhythm in the chest pressed against hers was steady and strong. Oddly, it soothed her. Her breathing evened out. Her sobs dissolved to a whisper in the back of her throat. Eyes closed, she felt his big hands ease their grip on her shoulders, sliding down her arms in calming strokes. Her limbs responded with a heaviness borne of exhaustion. She felt safe, protected.

"There's no reason to be afraid anymore," he whispered close to her ear. Another minute and the pads of his thumbs wiped the tears from her cheeks. Half asleep, she heard him talk to the wolf as he bandaged her hand and moved away from her side.

"Go to bed, Dood."

The big wolf climbed up beside her. Floating on the effects of the sedative Doc gave her, she wasn't afraid as Dood laid his head on her abdomen. He licked her hand as if sensing her distress, and she tumbled into a restful sleep.

By the time she awoke again, the sky glowed red with dusk. She glanced at the skylight above her head, and then at the big man overshadowing her bed. He tossed her shoulder bag to the mattress and signaled the wolf away from her.

"Get dressed. I'll be in the kitchen when you're ready. And don't make any side trips from here to the kitchen, unless it's to the bathroom. You don't want me coming after you."

"You're right about that," Melena mumbled to herself, wrapping the quilt around her as she eased over the side of the bed. Had she only imagined this gruff man calming her fears and telling her not to be afraid a few hours ago? Why was he so rough with her now?

Her legs felt like rubber, and shook with the effort, as she stumbled to the door. She dragged the purse behind her as she staggered across the hall to the bathroom. The taps worked when she turned on the shower this time. She adjusted the temperature and closed the glass door. As the hot spray pelted her aching muscles and the patchwork of bruises, pathetic moans escaped her throat.

For the first time in her life, she felt frightened and helpless. She had set the wheels in motion, put herself in this position by coming to the lake. Now she needed to get herself out of it before it was too late. She didn't know who the enemy was, but after her close brush with Campo this morning, she knew she was in real danger.

# Chapter 4

Theo pushed bacon and scrambled eggs around the pan on the stove when Melena's gut-wrenching whimpers filled the air. He wasn't immune. A woman's pain always got to him. This was no exception. He locked his knees where he stood. Otherwise, he'd be through that bathroom door, gathering her in his arms, and kissing the hurts away from her beautiful body.

Hell, he'd seen the marks of brutal assault marring her skin. Had it been a sexual attack? Could be, but he was inclined to believe it was more—maybe the means to an end—that of terrorizing her. Did someone else want in on the big payoff of Sarah Davidson's millions? Was the violence against Melena a falling out among murderers and thieves?

She appeared in the doorway a few minutes later, standing barefoot in a clean T-shirt and shorts. The tang of citrus and lemongrass surrounded her, the scent of her soap overpowering him like the kick from a stallion. *Jesus, Mary, and Joseph.* He clenched his jaw and stood his ground.

Dropping her shoulder bag to the floor with a thud, she crossed her arms over her chest in a protective gesture. Her irises were red-rimmed, her face devoid of makeup. Pale skin showcased the darkening bruise on her jaw, the oblong bandage at her hairline.

She wobbled where she stood. Only the rigidity of her spine, defiant angle of her chin, and diamond-sharp gaze kept her from looking like an assault victim. There was fight in her yet and he admired her for it.

"Whatever you're cooking, I'm not hungry."

He ignored her, brought the heaping plates to the table, and set them down. Picking up the coffee pot, he poured two cups. "Sit down before you fall down. I doubt you've eaten for at least twenty-four hours, maybe longer. That dizziness you're experiencing isn't from the injection Doc gave you. It's from lack of food."

"The only thing I need from you is a ride back to civilization. I came here on a fool's errand, to meet with a lawyer who has no intention of showing up. So, if you don't mind, just drive me back to the boat landing and my car."

Her breath hitched when she spoke, almost as if it was too much effort to get the words out. Still, she seemed determined to butt heads with him.

"After I've eaten."

Her fragility worried him. He reminded himself she could be a cold-blooded killer. Still, picking on her was like kicking a puppy. Where was the fun in that? Setting his cup down, Theo motioned to the place set across the table from him. If Melena didn't sit down soon, she would pass out and fall flat on her face. "You can plant yourself in that chair and wait until I'm finished."

Theo watched her shift her weight from one foot to the other, seemingly rooted to the floor in the entryway. Seeing her indecision, he spoke again between mouthfuls. "By the way, the lawyer has shown. That would be me."

"*You?*" She moved to the table, sank to the chair, and glared at him. "*You're* Theo Sauvage?"

"In the flesh, sugar." He shot a hand across the table and captured her trembling fingers in a mock handshake. "Theo Sauvage, Attorney at Law, at your service."

"What kind of game are you playing with me?" She eyed him warily. "*If* you're the lawyer, then why didn't you just tell me that last night? Why did you leave me here with that miserable wolf?"

Why indeed? *Maybe because you killed a good friend of mine?* "Because I had business to discuss with you, and I was too bloody-well tired to do it last night."

MELENA STARED AT HIM, aghast. The man was far too sexy, and dangerous looking, to be a lawyer. A pirate marauding the high seas, maybe, but definitely not a lawyer. Still, it made sense. She hadn't recognized his voice because his throat had been damaged in the car accident. "I don't even know you. What could you possibly have to discuss with me?"

"Eat your dinner, and then I'll tell you."

No sooner had she picked up a fork to manage a few mouthfuls, and he fired questions at her. "Who were those men on the boat today? What did they want with you?"

"I don't know, and I don't know."

Theo gave her a smile that didn't reach his eyes. "I hope you'll forgive me if I don't believe you?"

"Oh, for heaven's sake." She dropped the fork on her plate and stood to pace the room. Swaying slightly, she jabbed a finger in his direction. "I came to this lake at your request, if you remember. *You* could have hired those men to attack me, for all I know."

"Well, I could have, but I didn't. It's much more likely they followed you here."

He seemed to study her long and hard, as if gauging her reaction to his questions. She continued to pace, feeling like an animal trapped in his sights.

"What have you gotten yourself into, Mel? It looked to me like those guys meant serious business."

Temper flared and her fists swooped against the tabletop. The dishes vibrated. "Look, Mr. Hotshot Attorney, you know a lot more about what's going on around here than I do. So, why don't you enlighten me, and then we'll both know?"

Theo said nothing for several seconds. Instead, he moved to clear the dishes and replenish their coffee, splashing a generous portion of Irish Mist into both cups. He pulled an envelope from the top drawer of the hutch and tossed it like a gauntlet onto the table between them.

She picked up the envelope, taking in the spidery script with her name etched across the front of it. She gasped when he grabbed her wrist in a firm grip.

"You want to know what's going on? Read it and weep."

She pulled away from his hand to loosen the seal on the back of the envelope. "Why? Why should this make me weep?"

His gaze bore down on her. "Because it's a letter from beyond the grave. From a fine old lady who deserved far more at the end of her life than to be blown to kingdom come."

"My God, you're acting as if *I'm* responsible for her death." As the ugly realization dawned, Melena felt the blood drain from her face. "This woman was murdered, wasn't she?"

Theo shoved a cigar between clenched teeth and fired up, tossing the lighter to the table. "Yes, I'm convinced of it. Just read the letter and get it over with."

Mel swallowed the lump in her throat, slit open the envelope, and unfurled the pages. She read silently.

*My dearest Melena,*

*We have not met, nor will we meet, for I have instructed my attorney to deliver this to you only upon my death. There is no easy way to say this, so please forgive an old lady's bluntness. You are my granddaughter, dear, the daughter of my deceased son, Kenneth.*

*Please know that I wasn't aware of your existence until many years after your birth. I was heartbroken when I found out, but it was much too late to get you back. Your adopted family loved you so, and I knew in my soul you were better off with them.*

*Ken didn't see fit to confide in me in those days, not about your birth or about anything else in his life. He was barely out of high school when you were born. Yet, he was already on the fast track to trouble. And now he's gone. You, my darling, are all that is left of him.*

*Melena, I never contacted you in all these years because it would have been the wrong thing to do. Ken chose such a dark path for his short life. I was afraid there would be serious repercussions to you if anyone discovered you were his child. I simply could not trust them to leave you alone.*

*So please, darling, accept what little I can give you now and know you were always in my heart.*

*My lawyer, Theo Sauvage, can be trusted to see to your needs and inheritance. He is like a second son to me. Through the years, he has eased my burden of loving and losing Kenneth. Theo will take care of you because I wish it.*

*But, Melena, do* not *trust anyone else with the secret of your birth. For your sake, the past must die with me.*

*Your loving grandmother,*
*Sarah Davidson*

"I don't...how can...?"

She searched Theo's gaze as the blood drained from her head to her feet. The room whirled and she tumbled to the floor. The last thing she remembered before fainting was him gathering her in his arms, prying the pages from her hands and scanning them. The sound of his voice echoed from far, far away.

"Bloody hell."

### THE OUTSKIRTS OF LAS *Vegas, Nevada*

Tony gazed out the wall of glass to the panoramic vista of mountains shimmering in the distance while waiting for an audience with the old man. The miles of unforgiving desert surrounding this haven nudged verdant grasslands, a testament to the holdings and power of Angelo Vincelli and the cartel.

Watching thoroughbreds graze in pristine paddocks, gardeners trimming and coaxing rose bushes and hedges to life, Tony knew even the laws of nature bowed to Angelo Vincelli's billions. Yes, the old man still held the power from the glory days. But, it was Tony who managed the family's holdings now. It was also Tony who held the Harvard business degree and clarity of vision for the future of the casinos. The old ways of doing business were gone forever.

Or, they should have been.

Tony had first heard the rumblings about a contract killing through dependable sources in Canada. Instantly, Tony had known that even after all this time, the old man still wielded his personal brand of vengeance. His name was written all over the boat explosion. Angelo Vincelli had hired the hit on Sarah Davidson. There was no doubt about it.

Shoulders stooped with resignation, Tony waited to confront the old man. Angelo wasn't going to let the past stay buried where it belonged. His foolishness risked bringing the entire cartel to its knees. Tony couldn't let it happen. The question was what, if anything, could be done about it? To Angelo Vincelli, Tony was still his child and would be treated as a child. Hell, even Tony didn't want to incur the wrath of the powerful Vincelli Don.

"Well, well. I didn't expect to see you today." Angelo entered the room by a recessed entry in a rear wall panel. He bypassed his massive mahogany desk and leather chair for the window grouping of club chairs where Tony sat. At seventy-two, Angelo was still a big man with a full head of silver hair, a piercing blue-eyed gaze, and an imposing presence. He was dressed for business in a charcoal Armani suit. Gold cufflinks winked in the sunlight, as did the chunky signet ring he'd worn for as long as Tony could remember.

Angelo reached for the humidor and withdrew a Cuban cigar. He inhaled its scent before clipping the end and lighting a match, softly puffing. "It isn't often you come out this far just to see your old man. Tell me; to what do I owe the pleasure?"

Tony fidgeted in the chair, feeling like a scared rabbit about to be torn apart by a predator. However, this had to be said. This had to end now, for the sake of the family business.

"How could you think I wouldn't find out? And how can you justify hiring a hit on Sarah Davidson, Papa? She was a helpless old lady, for pity's sake."

"What? You think you're giving the orders now? Is that it?" Angelo's wrath took hold in the blink of an eye. "Let me make something crystal clear to you. *You* are nothing to this organization but a lousy pencil pusher. And you only hold that position as long as I say so."

He waived his cigar in the air as he spoke. "Yeah, you do good for the legit side of the family business. But you know nothing about how the Vincelli name came to be respected and feared."

Tony leaned forward in the chair. "Papa, I just want you to listen to reason."

"No. You listen to me, because I am only going to say this once." Angelo blew smoke in the air and stubbed out the smouldering cigar for emphasis. "There are grey areas in this business, Tony, and there are black areas. I haven't pushed you enough in those directions. But, that stops now.

Angelo's gaze intensified as the tone of his voice become very low. "Ken Davidson took what was mine and made a fool of me. While I paid for his funeral and prayed over his grave, the jerk-off was still alive. He retired a very rich man on *my* money. No one steals from me and lives to talk about it. *No one.*"

"But Papa..."

"Just shut the hell up and pay attention. Ken Davidson is *alive*, Tony. I'm going to smoke that traitor out and make an example of him. Yeah, killing his mama was only the beginning for good old Kenny. It seems he has a daughter, some bastard kid he gave up before he came to work for the cartel. She's resurfaced. And you're going to grab her, Tony. Then you're going to bring her to me. Because—if you don't—your aspirations of ever running this organization will be cut off at the knees. Ba-da-bing, ba-da-boom."

Tony stiffened and seethed with hatred. *That's typical of you, you prick. You don't get what you want and you'll take away my dreams for the family business? Hell will freeze over first, old man.* "I understand, Papa."

"I figured you would. Now go home and pack. You're leaving tonight on a flight for Montreal with a crew who I've handpicked. You'll be met at the other end by our people up there. You find Melena Salera—that's the name she uses. Then you bring the sacrificial lamb home to your papa."

# Chapter 5

Melena awoke with a groan and kicked the sheets to the floor before rolling out of bed. She had a headache, a huge Irish Mist headache. After locking Theo out last night, she had drowned her sorrows in doctored coffees—too many to count. Caffeine zinged through her veins like a wild thing this morning, her heart bouncing in her chest like a tennis ball on speed.

Worse than that, her family's betrayal had leeched into her soul. Fissures of hurt had widened to an overflowing river of despair that threatened to rip her apart.

How could her parents have kept such a huge secret from her? Was it beneath their social standing to admit they had adopted their only child? Or had they kept silent for another reason?

She doubted it. Her mother had devoted her entire adult life to furthering her husband's career within the government hierarchy. Melena had tried to track her parents down last night on her cell phone. They hadn't picked up. She knew they were travelling in Haiti right now as part of a good will mission, but would be back in Ottawa next week for a dinner with the Prime Minister. If they didn't return her call before then, she'd make the drive to Ottawa.

*I'll be at the airport to greet them when their plane touches down. "Hello, Mother and Father. By the way, were you ever going to tell me I'm adopted?"*

"Adopted..." She could hardly say the word, yet she knew it was true. So many things clicked into place with that realization. She had always felt out of place in her parents' home. Their way of thinking was worlds apart from hers. She had never understood how she could be so different from them.

Massaging a temple, she downed a couple of aspirin with a glass of juice. She still had so many unanswered questions. She thought her brain might split apart like her broken heart.

Hitting the bedroom floor, she launched into a series of push-ups and sit-ups, gritting her teeth to keep her wounded psyche at bay. Straining and flexing until sweat slicked her body, she soon lost count of the repetitions.

She ached for her younger self. A little girl left in boarding schools on holidays while her father's duties carried her parents to foreign lands for weeks, sometimes months, at a time. During those times of abandonment, there had been a grandmother who could have played a major role in her life. Yet, her grandmother had chosen to remain on the sidelines. *Why?*

Now, it was too late. She would never know Sarah Davidson, and never understand why her biological family had broken that bond of caring for their own flesh and blood. Instead, she had been handed over to strangers to be raised. Or were they strangers?

It wasn't that Melena didn't love her family. She did, wholeheartedly. Still, to be a child tossed aside by her real family tainted every childhood memory she possessed. Her biological family hadn't wanted her. *Why not?*

She understood. Her birth father and grandmother were dead and couldn't provide answers to her questions. But, what about her mother and her side of the family? Where were they? *Surely there's someone, somewhere, who can explain things to me?*

She would find out the truth. It was her right to know. If the lawyer wasn't willing to help, then she would look elsewhere. Theo wasn't the only game in town. If she needed to hire a detective to find the answers, she damn well would.

CODY ANSWERED THE PHONE on the third ring. "It's about time you called. I'll get Sully on the line as soon as he stops kissing my mom. It's really getting embarrassing, you know? A muscle-bound cop like him making goo-goo eyes every time he looks at her."

Sully's future son was thirteen going on thirty, a dynamite teen who had Theo's brother wrapped around his little finger. He had narrowly escaped death a week earlier when the psycho had gone after his mother in Mallard Bay. They all thanked God the boy seemed none the worse for his ordeal.

"I know, big guy, it must be tough to watch, but that's what love does to a man."

"No kidding, Theo. It's turning his brain to mush. I guess the bigger they are, the harder they really do fall. I don't want a girl in my life for at least fifty more years if that's what happens. Hold on while I see if 'hot lips' can come up for air."

Thirty seconds later, Sully chuckled on the other end of the line. "What's up? Are there any new developments on the case?"

"Yes, Sarah's body has been released. The funeral is scheduled for tomorrow at one. Can you make it?"

"Only if you're sure you want to be invaded, bro. I have some time off and so does Breeana. Plus, Mom and Dad flew in last night from San Antonio. How do you feel about all of us crashing with you for a while?"

"Hey, I'll look forward to it. Tell Cody to bring a friend with him if he wants. There's a lot for a kid to do here if he's got someone to hang with."

"I'll do that."

"By the way, you'll never guess what was in the letter Sarah left for Melena Salera."

Theo quickly filled Sully in on the details, as well as the attack on her by the thugs in the boat.

"That does put a whole new slant on things. The woman could be another victim."

"I'm not convinced. It could also be a falling out among thieves. What if she already knew Sarah was her grandmother? There are a lot of websites with a wealth of information for an adoptee looking for her birth family. She could be one terrific actress, and guilty of killing Sarah."

"Maybe." Sullivan was silent for a moment. "Looks like we're right back where we started. I'll get my hands on a copy of the autopsy report and bring it with me tomorrow."

"Sounds good. See you then."

The call disconnected and Theo tossed the phone to a cushioned deck chair. He thought about Melena. She hadn't spoken another word to him last night after reading Sarah's letter. In fact, she had booted him out of the house once he had scraped her off the floor and she got her second wind. He almost felt guilty for giving her such a hard time over Sarah's death. Almost, but not quite.

A SINGLE PIPER CROSSED in front of the tombstones; the sad sound of bagpipes filled the air then floated out across the valley overlooking Silver Lake.

*Amazing Grace.*

The cemetery at the back of the old clapboard church was picture perfect. A park sat to the side of the building, complete with a white arbor where the reception would be held after the service. The sun shone and blue jays swooped in a cloudless sky. Sarah's casket was on the platform above her final resting place, green carpet edging the brass poles surrounding the coffin. It was silly, really, but Melena thought her grandmother would be peaceful resting here.

She wanted to cry. She hugged her arms around herself instead. Any tears she shed would be for the wrong reasons. Because of the hymn, or because she felt sorry for herself and all the time she'd missed with her grandmother. Try as she might, she couldn't bring herself to grieve for someone she hadn't known.

Theo performed the eulogy and a minister led the congregation in prayer. People were invited to the podium to talk about Sarah, her life and their love for her. All the while, friends passed before her coffin to pay their final respects. Many laid flowers on top.

Melena didn't have a flower to give. She didn't have any words to say, any stories to share. She stood in front of the casket smelling the upturned earth. How long she stayed there she didn't know. She studied the picture on an easel of the vibrant, smiling woman who had been her flesh and blood. Did she resemble her grandmother? It was impossible to tell.

But, one thing was clear. Sarah Davidson had been resilient. She had overcome incredible sadness in her life to become a friend to these people who mourned her. The laugh lines and sparkling green eyes in her photo revealed as much.

The mourners were watching Melena, weighing her reaction as she said her goodbyes and moved back into the crowd. She sensed the scrutiny. Not just Theo's from the podium but others as well. Many of Sarah's friends had guessed she was the woman's granddaughter. What did they think of her? Did they believe she was somehow to blame?

Theo certainly did. He hardly took his eyes off her during the service. Cold eyes, resentful eyes that accused. She almost couldn't blame him. His grief was palpable. His desolate gaze, the hard clench of his jaw just about did her in. She wanted to reach out, touch him, and tell him how sorry she was for his loss. He would never accept it. Not from her.

"He's all right," a voice whispered beside her. "He'll grieve, but he'll move on. Don't feel sad for him."

Melena turned to the striking woman beside her and whispered, "I'm sorry, but have we met?"

"Karine Sauvage, dear. Theo's mother. He's known Sarah since he was a little boy. He has so many happy memories of her. Have him share those with you, Melena."

"Why would I do that?" she asked, twisting Sarah's gold Celtic ring around her finger. She'd found it in her jewelry box and slipped it on, wanting to feel close to her. The worn design of the cross was smooth against her skin.

"So you can grieve for your grandmother." Karine patted her arm. "You should get to know her. She was so proud of you."

"You're wrong about that. My grandmother didn't know me at all."

"Of course, she did. She knew you very well. I attended a couple of your ballet recitals myself. Remember when you played a mouse in Cinderella?"

Melena nodded, perplexed. "I was four years old."

"That's right," Karine said. "The first concert your grandma took me to. She was there for every milestone in your life, you know."

Warmed by Karine's generosity, Melena swallowed her sorrow. It was too late for her. Too late to get to know her grandmother.

There was a loud cough from the podium and Karine stopped talking. Melena looked up and saw Theo giving her the evil eye. His glare told her all she needed to know. He wasn't happy to see her with his mother. Rather than cause problems between them, she excused herself and disappeared into the crowd.

Another pair of eyes followed her retreat.

A laser-beam stare drilled into the back of her head. It wasn't Theo's, not unless he'd moved from the podium. A shiver ghosted her spine. She spun around and saw one of the men who attacked her, the one they called Campo. He stood in the shadows off to the side, beneath a giant maple tree.

Their gazes met. Campo mimicked a slash across his throat, pointed to her then turned and walked into the forest edging the cemetery.

Melena wanted to scream at the threat. She hurried to the spot where she'd seen him go through the trees then slowed her steps. Apprehension tempered her initial reaction. She might feel like a crazy woman, but not enough to follow him into a trap. Anger was one thing, stupidity another.

As she stared after him, a horrible thought took shape in her mind. She stood stock still, clenching then unclenching her hands. Maybe she was just being paranoid.

*Is it possible Campo killed my grandmother?*

# Chapter 6

Theo nursed a beer after the funeral, relieved he'd gotten through the eulogy without his voice cracking. Honoring Sarah's life and her accomplishments was the least he could do for her. He lifted his pilsner glass in a silent toast.

He avoided talking to his family, was still irritated at his mother for chatting with Melena during the service. What did they have to talk about? A big fat nothing, as far as he knew.

Melena. He'd watched her like a hawk all afternoon, half expecting her to cry crocodile tears over Sarah's coffin, or pull some other emotional nonsense to get the sympathy vote from Sarah's friends. She hadn't, which surprised him.

His gaze cut to her now as she collected plastic glasses, cutlery and paper plates off the grass and shoved them into a garbage bag. She looked pale and gaunt, as if the day had proven tough. He grabbed another garbage bag and moved to help her.

"I'll take you back to the cottage when we're finished."

She scarcely glanced at him. "No thanks. Doc and Effie brought me and they promised to take me home."

"Home, already, is it? Didn't take you long to stake your claim, sugar."

"It is what it is, Theo." She blew out a breath, clutching the garbage bag in front of her like a shield. "My grandmother chose to give me the cottage. Wouldn't she want me to think of it as home?"

"She'd *want* to still be alive."

"You're acting as if it's my fault she's dead." Melena stared at him for several seconds. "Campo was at the funeral today. I think he killed her."

"Really? And did you hire him to do it?"

She landed the punch to his gut before he saw it coming. "God damn!"

"Enjoy your beer and hallucinations," Melena whispered, a snarl in her tone. "I'm done here."

Palms planted on his knees, Theo gulped air, watched her spin on her heels and head for Effie and Doc. In spite of himself, he couldn't help but admire her tush in the tailored skirt as she stomped through the grass, making a beeline for the boat dock.

He rubbed his hand over his lower abs, over the spot where she'd slugged him.

*Happy now, hot shot? You pushed her too far and got exactly what you deserved.*

"HEY, WILL YOU LOOK at that? Two babes on windsurfers and one of them just tipped over." Cody winked at his buddy Pierre and eyeballed his future uncle. "Can we borrow one of your kickass boats to go to the rescue?"

Theo glanced at Breeana for confirmation that Cody could even drive a boat. They were sitting high above the water, out on the sundeck that wrapped around the glass and wood structure of his island retreat. Sully had just ducked inside for drinks. Breeana, dressed in a sleek black swimsuit, was settled on a chaise longue with a bottle of sunscreen and a great book, a crime-buster his sister had written.

Theo noted, not for the first time, that Breeana McGill was an incredibly beautiful woman—a sizzling, green-eyed, redhead with the temperament to match. His brother had lucked out when he rescued her from the clutches of a madman. She was every man's fantasy. Almost. She wasn't *his* fantasy. No, his preferences ran toward icy baby-blues and one spitfire blond wrapped up in a compact, delicious package. Melena Salera was the poster girl for his kind of woman, the kind who made him ache bone-deep.

Whoa...sex was one thing. But, commitment was something he absolutely did not want, or need. Would he be able to keep the two separate with Melena? The thought scored a direct hit to his solar plexus. She could be guilty of killing Sarah. What in hell was he thinking?

Ms. Salera spent entirely too much time at the forefront of his thoughts, especially since the funeral yesterday. Was she guilty of killing Sarah? Or, was she innocent? He couldn't seem to decide.

The sun was over the yardarm. A cold beer would feel mighty fine going down right about now, if his brother ever came out of the house with the brew in question. It might help get his mind off the unsettling stirrings he felt for his suspect.

Breeana lowered her sunglasses to study him over the tops of her lenses. He realized he had zoned out of the conversation around him.

"Theo? Cody's got his boater's license," she said. "He couldn't very well grow up on Lac St-Louis and not learn to drive a boat."

"Okay then." Theo refocused, straightening in his chair and pointing down to the dock. "Take that small fishing boat, Cody, the one I call my tin can. And you guys remember to wear your life vests."

"No problem."

Within minutes, the boys could be seen out on the sparkling waves, flirting with the two pretty girls who seemed to be about their age. The girls were *oohing* and *aahing* over Cody's golden retriever and rottweiler, while Cody and Pierre basked in the limelight. They wouldn't be home for hours.

"Ah, to be young again." Theo sighed, envying the boys. *It would be nice not to think about murder and one sexy murder suspect in particular.*

Sully appeared on deck with three frosties and the autopsy report on Sarah Davidson tucked under an arm. After handing over the beers, he slid Breeana's legs aside and flopped down beside her, passing the file folder to Theo. Grabbing the sunscreen, he smoothed it on Breeana's shoulders and arms. One of her hands was wrapped in a cast, a painful reminder of her recent brush with death.

Mom and Pop chose that moment to amble up from the dock. Theo thought the family resemblance between his father, Sully and him was undeniable. Pop had an athletic build and worked hard to maintain it. With a full head of silver-streaked hair and a dark, penetrating gaze, he was a powerhouse. Yet, he knew it was his mother who held the real authority. Tall and slender, with warm chestnut hair and eyes the color of smoke, she could control the family's unruly behavior with little more than a raised eyebrow.

Sully returned to the kitchen to grab a few more beers while Theo dragged two more deck chairs into their group. Returning with the drinks and passing them out, Sully plunked himself down beside Breeana again and took a swallow from his own mug.

"You and Doc Finley were right, bro. Sarah had a truckload of roofies in her system on the night her boat exploded. Not only is Rohypnol a tranquilizer, it's a muscle relaxant that reduces the psychomotor responses to almost nil. In other words, there is no way she could have even been standing, let alone driving the boat that night."

"Shit." Theo quickly scanned through the pages in front of him. "So, whoever drugged Sarah tossed her into that boat, aimed it toward the rocks, and gunned the throttle. The perp must have hauled ass overboard before the crash."

"That's about the size of it. So, where does that leave us in the investigation?"

"It could point back to Melena Salera," Theo surmised. "I did some digging into her background. She works for a pharmaceutical company as a sales trainer. She's no doubt got access to Rohypnol."

"Not unless her company is the manufacturer," Breeana offered. "I would have better access by placing an order through the clinic, since it is sold legally as a veterinary sedative. Otherwise, I don't think it's a widely prescribed drug used for legitimate purposes."

"Breeana's right," his father intervened. "Besides, roofies are available on the street to almost anyone, Theo, right alongside the so-called designer drugs. It's known as the date rape drug."

"I'm still not convinced she wasn't involved, Pop. When Melena was attacked the other morning out on the water, it could have been a settling of accounts. Maybe she put the wheels in motion to have Sarah eliminated and then decided not to pay up."

"You can't seriously believe that. Why are you being so hard on this girl?" His mother sent him a challenging stare, glancing briefly at his father for support. "I met her at the funeral yesterday and she seems to be a genuine, caring person. I can't believe she would harm her grandmother."

"Not even for the multimillion-dollar payoff?" Theo studied his parents as the light bulb went on in his head. They were holding out on him. He could feel it. "Look, I'm starting to realize you know more about this woman than you're letting on. What aren't you telling me?"

His father drained his glass, leaned forward in his chair, and raked a palm across his chin. "Son, I was Sarah's close friend and her attorney for many years before you took over my law practice. And yes, your mother and I were aware Sarah had a granddaughter. She told us about Melena when she first began tracking her whereabouts. I helped her do it. We were sworn to secrecy, Theo, and we simply couldn't tell anyone. Sarah's murder, now that changes a whole lot of things. But, the bottom line is your mother and I believe Melena is innocent of any wrongdoing in this."

"How can you be so sure she's innocent?" Theo's gaze narrowed on his father. "And why all the secrecy about Sarah's grandchild in the first place?"

"It had something to do with Kenneth, Sarah's son. She never divulged the details, not even to me. I only know Sarah feared harm would come to Melena if anyone found out about her. And before you ask, we don't know who her mother is.

"You can't be sure she's guilty, Theo. Stop being so mule-headed about her and start doing some real digging."

Theo focused on his father, not liking where this conversation was headed. The apple didn't fall far from the tree where Pop and he were concerned. They were both capable of digging in their heels and staying on opposite sides of this fence.

"Look, I have an idea," Sully offered. "Why don't we just ask her what she knows? I'd like to interview the lady, bro, and I couldn't very well do it at the funeral yesterday."

Breeana winked at Theo and smooched Sully square on the lips. "Hey, that's a lovely idea, Lieutenant. I'd like to meet this gal myself, since she's got your brother tied up in knots. Why don't we take a short nap while the boys are still occupied with the damsels in distress? Then we can pay Melena a visit."

"I love the way your mind works, cookie." Sully tapped her lightly on the temple after giving an exaggerated yawn. "We'll be ready to go in an hour, bro, after we grab some shut-eye."

"Yeah, sure," Theo snorted. "I'll be down swimming some laps until then. I wouldn't want to hear the two of you snoring."

"Ahem. Your father and I will stay here and keep an eye on the boys when you go over to Melena's," his mother offered. "I think we can handle anything Cody and Pierre come up with while you're gone."

"That's right. Take your time while we hold down the fort with the boys." Pop reached for his wife and pulled her to her feet. "Meanwhile, let's join Theo for a dip in the lake, dear."

Theo grunted, whipped off his shirt and hopped over the deck rail. He jackknifed off the rocks into the bay without a backward glance at his family. His body cleaved the water and leveled out.

Alone with his thoughts, he stayed submerged until rounding a bend of shoreline when anger propelled him to the surface like a cork popping from a champagne bottle. Water sluiced off his hair and shoulders as he struck out across the waves with powerful strokes. He would muscle his way through this crazy obsession he had with Melena.

*Dumb ass, you could be with her right now if you weren't so fixated on her guilt or innocence. You've finessed your way with women more times than you can count. So, why should this one be any different?*

Because he cared about her on a deeper level, he acknowledged, in spite of her potential involvement in Sarah's murder. *Damn.* How asinine was that? He needed to uncover the truth—fast—and screw his head on straight while he was at it.

It was beyond him why Mom and Pop thought her above suspicion. Sully seemed to waffle on the subject as well since laying eyes on her at the funeral. Maybe they were right. Still, what could they see other than a pretty face and beguiling nature?

His own instincts had always served him well. Those same instincts warned him; there was a lot more to Melena than her obvious physical appeal. She held the key to Sarah's murder, of that he was sure. Was she guilty or just a pawn in the game? More importantly, would he get to know her better? Or drop-kick her to prison once the evidence was in?

MELENA SAT IN THE BOATHOUSE in the little runabout that had been Sarah's backup transportation. The motor wouldn't start. Frustrated, she ran through the checklist from the boat engine manual she had found stashed under the seat.

Was there gas and oil in the tank? Check.

Was the fuel line connected properly to both the tank and the 15 HP motor? Check again.

Had she squeezed the bulb on the fuel line to push gas up into the engine? Triple check.

The gear shift was in neutral, the throttle turned to the start position, and the choke knob was pulled wide open. So, why didn't the blasted thing start when she pulled on the starter cable? Her arm already ached from several pulls on the stupid thing. What the heck was the problem?

What she wanted—no, what she *needed*—was to be independent. That meant learning to drive and maintain this blasted boat which was her only method of transport on the lake. While Doc Finley and his wife had come by to take her to the funeral yesterday, Melena knew she could not be dependent on other people's generosity. Not if she wanted to put her plan into action and remain at the lake for the next few months.

Yes, she intended to stick around, learn more about her family and the skeletons in their closet. Truth be told, she had already fallen in love with Silver Lake and her inherited cottage. But, she couldn't stay if she couldn't get the damn motor started and figure out this boating thing.

Independence meant everything to her; Theo Sauvage be damned. She didn't need him or his insinuation that she had murdered her grandmother.

She also didn't need his bedroom eyes or his yummy, ripped body. That's right. She could ignore her built-in hunk-o-meter. She could be tough. Sure, it soared off the charts whenever he was within range, but so what? The you're-a-big-jerk-for-thinking-I-killed-my grandmother-meter whooped every time he came near her, too.

He was supposed to be her lawyer, for heaven's sake. What happened to innocent until proven guilty? Theo was one dangerous bad-boy she would avoid in the future at all costs.

Gritting her teeth, she yanked again on the starter cable, swearing as the motor again sputtered and died.

"See what the trouble is?"

The voice came from the shadows of the boathouse. Melena knew that voice. Campo. She hadn't heard him coming. Her heart beat like a jackhammer. She scrambled for the side of the boat to dive overboard. Too late. Campo dropped down in the seat beside her before she could move. Seizing her arm, he wrenched it behind her back.

"The kill switch is still engaged because I removed the safety clip. That's why the motor wouldn't start, you dumb bitch."

Dangling the safety from his free hand, he tossed it over the side. Melena's skin crawled, repelled by his touch, just as her body trembled at the obvious intent in his eyes. He had come to finish the job from the other morning.

She tightened her grip on the metal flashlight still in her hand from verifying the mixture in the gas tank. Metal struck bone with a sickening crunch as she lashed out at Campo's face. He reeled to the side as cartilage cracked and blood spurted from his nose.

His hand dropped away from her arm and Melena lunged for the pier. Her knees slammed the planking as her feet skidded out from under her. She ignored the pain and scrambled to her feet, sprinting for the boathouse doorway and freedom.

Someone tripped her when she cleared the arch, pitching her face-down on the graveled path. Melena gasped with pain as she rolled to avoid the punt from a booted foot. The other men from the previous attack loomed over her. They blocked out the sun, thwarting any chance of escape. Their gazes travelled her length, intentions clear on their shadowed faces. Her entire body clenched with terror. *Holy God!*

"We got her."

The bigger man reached down, clamped her around the waist, and whipped her off the ground. The third man's hands groped her. Her T-shirt ripped as the men sandwiched her between them. Frantic now, Melena lashed out, kicking with both feet. There was no power behind those thrusts, her knees battered from smashing into the wharf. She screamed until her throat was hoarse, twisted and turned in a desperate struggle to get their hands off her.

Campo stomped out of the boathouse, swiped at his bloody nose with a bare arm, and nudged her hard. "Shut the hell up."

The bigger man held her fast, laughed at her useless attempts to free herself. "Can we do her now, Campo? She's a frigging hellcat. There's enough fight in her for all of us."

Melena saw stars as Campo grabbed her by the nape, wrenched her away from his sidekicks, and licked the side of her face. He stank like a feral animal. "You like rough sex, baby?"

His bulging crotch prodded her stomach. He clutched her hair in his fists while he tasted her neck. His rancid breath puffed against her. Blood from his nose smeared her skin as he angled his mouth toward her cleavage."

She bit down hard on his ear, jerked a knee up with all her strength, and scored a direct hit between his legs. "Drop dead."

Campo released his hold then doubled in agony. He dropped to his knees, gripping himself through the front of his jeans. Melena leaped over him and tore for the woods like a sprinter at the starter pistol. The others caught her within seconds, rough hands biting into her flesh while Campo recovered from the blow. Straightening again, he slammed into her ribs with an angry punch.

"You'll pay for that. You should have taken the hint and gone home while you still had the chance." Melena tasted bile. She sagged with pain when Campo hoisted her over his shoulder and struck out along the path for the cabin. "I'm gonna show you how a *real* man treats a woman."

Her breath came out in short gasps, the pressure of his shoulder to her midsection cutting off her air supply. She raised herself with her elbows to ease the pressure.

"I don't know, man," the smaller man trailing behind her said. "The boss said to bring her to him. We don't have time to mess around."

"Shut your cake-hole, Jean-Guy. The boss isn't here and I'm the one giving the orders. If you don't want a piece of her, you can keep watch while me and Roger have us some fun. Besides, the boss won't care what condition she's in when he gets her."

Jean-Guy didn't have time to get another word out before Melena saw Doodlebug launch through the trees. One minute, the thug was directly behind her on the path. The next minute, he was gaping up from the ground, gurgling sounds escaping his lips. Dood released him and leapt for Roger. It was over in another instant. The wolf growled viciously, turning his attention on Campo.

Campo dumped her on the path and pulled a gun from his waistband. He fired. The shots rang out as Dood soared through the air then dropped like a stone. Seconds passed as the stench of cordite swirled around them. Melena sobbed, not for the dead men, but for the wolf that had defended her with his life.

Campo barely glanced at the carnage. He snagged her by the wrists and dragged her the rest of the way along the path, up the stairs, and into the house. "It's your fault I lost those men. And believe me, you're gonna pay for that too."

# Chapter 7

"Gunfire." Theo yelled over the thrust of the engine as he reached for the Glock 17 stored in the Bayliner's glove box.

Sully reacted by pulling his own weapon from an ankle holster strapped under his chinos. "The sound's distorted. Where's it coming from?"

"Close by. Too close." Theo pulled into Sarah's boathouse and quickly reversed thrust, cutting the engine. "Mel's got company."

"Shit." Sully briefly squeezed Breeana's arm as he leapt for the dock. "Stay in the boat. Don't you move!"

Theo barely paid attention to the bodies strewn on the path, other than to confirm neither was a female. His focus was on the open doorway of the cottage. He needed to find Melena fast. Sully guarded his six while they moved toward the cabin, until he signaled his brother to go around back.

Theo leapt onto the porch and watched for shadows inside the entrance. A head-on charge was potential suicide, but he had to take the risk. Melena was in danger, maybe hurt or dying. That's all he cared about. He crouched, somersaulted through the entryway and landed on his feet, listening for any signs of disturbance coming from the back rooms.

He heard something...a muffled sound...a sobbing intake of breath. Sweat slicked the grip of his weapon as he swung it in a firing stance, inched his way up the hallway, his back to a wall. One well placed kick and the bathroom door flew from its frame. What he saw after that shredded his insides to pieces. Melena trembled in the corner, her clothes torn and her lower lip bloody. She was alone. She was alive. She needed him.

Theo laid his Glock aside as he gathered her firmly against him. "Easy, I've got you."

She struggled to break his hold. "Quit fighting me, Mel. No one's going to hurt you. It's over now."

She blinked up at him, her body quaking. She thudded her fists against his chest. "What took you so long? I was scared to death."

"Nag. Nag. Nag." Theo relaxed slightly and bent to kiss the top of her head. His knees shook. At least his heart no longer threatened to pump from his chest. Melena was alive. That's all that mattered.

Hearing a sound from the hallway, he tensed, snatched up his Glock, and pointed it at the man crossing the bathroom threshold. His brother. He swung the barrel and pointed to the floor.

"A boat took off from the swimming dock. I couldn't get there in time to stop it. Whoever it was, he's gone."

Theo shielded Melena from Sully's view. "Give us a few minutes."

"Is she all right?"

"Hell no, she's not all right. The bastards beat her."

"I'll get Doc. I'm taking Breeana there now. There's a wolf outside that's been shot and left for dead. Bree says she can save him if we hurry. Doesn't Doc have a surgery set up at his place?"

"Yeah, he does. Tell Bree the wolf's name is Dood, Doodlebug. He belonged to Sarah. Just get Doc back here as fast as you can."

"You got it."

THEO PACED THE FLOOR while waiting for Doc to finish examining Melena in the bedroom. He should be outside with Sully explaining to the cops what had happened, but his focus was on Melena right now. Besides, Sully was a homicide lieutenant from Montreal and would be accorded professional courtesy by the local police. He'd have the bodies and police officers on their way in a fraction of the time it would take Theo. And he didn't want Melena bothered with questions. She'd been attacked and Dood had protected her, end of story. The facts would speak for themselves.

By the time Doc came out of the bedroom, he was ready to jump out of his skin. "What's the verdict, Doc?"

"She was lucky, although I doubt she's feeling that way right now. Lots more scrapes and contusions, but she's strong and will mend."

Theo nodded then forced out the question burning a hole in his gut for the last half hour. "Was she raped?"

"She says not, Theo." Doc sighed heavily. "It's lucky you showed up when you did."

*Some luck.*

He brought her tea laced with brandy and sank down beside her on the bed. She wasn't sleeping, only staring up through the skylight. She looked so lost and small in that big bed. "Talk to me, Mel."

He thought she might not say anything, yet he hoped she trusted him enough.

"It was Campo who shot Dood and got away. The others were Jean-Guy and Roger. I don't know their last names. I think their boss sent Campo and his men to kidnap me." A single tear found its way down her cheek. She scrubbed it away, her only sign of weakness. "Anyway, why should I tell you anything? You think I killed my grandmother. You don't care about me. Just go away and leave me alone."

She rolled away from him, her spine taut with tension.

"Please, sugar." Theo knew she was right. He hadn't believed her. He had allowed this to happen. "I was wrong about you. I acted like a complete jerk. But, no matter how you feel about me, I *am* going to help you. Tell me exactly what happened."

She turned in his direction and stared into his eyes for the longest time, as if judging the honesty there. She seemed to make the decision to trust him, at least temporarily.

"Campo was angry with me because I smashed him in the face with a flashlight. He said they were going to show me how real men did it. That's when the small man, Jean-Guy, started to panic. He told Campo the boss wouldn't like them hanging around, that the boss had told them to bring me to him."

"We were still struggling on the path when Dood charged out of the woods. He killed Jean-Guy. Then he attacked Roger. That's when Campo threw me to the ground, pulled his gun, and shot Doodlebug. After that, he dragged me up to the house, hauled me inside, and pulled me down the hall to the bedroom. When he heard your boat pull in, he took his eyes off me for a second. I ran into the bathroom and locked the door."

Her voice dwindled to nothing as she fought to stay in control. Theo was at a loss and did the only thing he knew to do. He reached out and gathered her to him. Hell, he wanted to make love to her, to make her forget. He knew the last thing she needed was another man crawling all over her. So, he fought the primal urge to take her as a lover, to mark her with his brand. Instead, he vowed in silence that no man would put his hands on her again, not unless she wanted to be touched.

He smoothed the hair off her forehead, his hand shaking. "Mel, I know you told Doc you weren't raped, but I have to ask again."

"No...I wasn't...raped."

He heaved a sigh of relief. He would get her through this. He would find out what in God's name was going on while he kept his raging hormones firmly under lock and key. "Congratulations on smashing Campo with that flashlight, by the way."

Melena managed a watery smile. "Next time, I'll carry a Taser to fry his testicles."

"Ouch. There won't be a next time, so don't worry about it." He stretched out beside her, nestled her bottom between his thighs, and pulled the quilt over her. "Close your eyes and go to sleep. I'm right here, and I'm not leaving."

She gasped, no doubt because his erection pulsed against her bottom with a mind of its own. Yeah, he wanted her, all right, but the timing was lousy. She had taken one hell of a beating, had almost been raped and killed. Besides, Doc had given her pain medication. She would be out like a light soon.

Turning in his arms, she peeked up at him. "Why do you carry a gun?"

*Damn, how much should I tell her?* "Well, it was one of the tools of the trade when I was in Special Ops. But, I'm a lawyer now."

"So, why do you still carry a weapon?"

*Yeesh.* He really did not want to get into this with her. What could he say? That his old team was now a reserve unit? That he was hauled out of mothballs from time to time?

*See, sugar, I'm still a highly classified killer for the military. That's right, I'm a sniper in my other life, and I have terrorist enemies who could pop out of the woodwork unexpectedly at any time.*

"Look, Mel, it's no big deal. I'm licensed to carry a concealed weapon, and that's all you need to know. The same goes for my brother, Sully. He's a homicide lieutenant, and he's always armed, especially since his fiancée and her son were attacked. But, for what it's worth, my brother and I are former armed forces and still attached to a Special Ops reserve unit. I can't discuss any of the details."

"In other words, I should mind my own business..." Melena's words slowed as the pain meds invaded her system. "Doodlebug...can he be saved?"

"Definitely, if I know my future sister-in-law. Breeana's a terrific vet. She'll give everything she's got to keep him alive."

Satisfied, Melena nodded, closed her eyes and was asleep within seconds. Theo couldn't tear his gaze away from her. He burned with the need to kill Campo, the only man left alive who had put his hands on her and filled her with terror.

He would find him and finish him. But first, he needed to find out who he worked for, and who was behind Sarah's death. Of course, his close proximity to Melena and his "hands off" policy might very well kill him before he got his chance.

"VINCELLI?" RICO POUNDED on the gymnasium door. One of Angelo's henchmen from Vegas, he was there to make sure Tony got the job done. "Pick up the phone. It's Angelo."

"Give me a minute." Completing a bench press, Tony hooked the barbell back on the rack, sat on the bench for a second mopping up sweat, then grabbed the phone. "Yeah, Papa."

"Idiot! You were supposed to call me hours ago," Angelo barked. "Where the hell've you been?"

Per usual, a conversation with Don Vincelli quickly became a screaming match. With him doing the screaming. "Where have *I* been? How about where has *Campo* been? We waited two hours at the airport for him and his crew to show up. They never came."

"Quit wasting time. Get out there and find them. They'll lead you to the woman."

"The hell I will. There's nothing but trees and bears for miles. I'm stuck in a lodge halfway up a mountainside, for God's sake. Scenic view, my butt. I've got better things to do right now, like finding Salera myself."

"You'll do as I say, you hear? Did you ever stop to think Campo could beat you to the prize? I told you, I want to deal with her myself. No one else pulls the trigger. Not you. Not Campo."

"Well, you should have thought of that before you hired the fool in the first place. He's got no loyalty to you. He's nothing but muscle for hire. What if he tries for her again and misses like he did the first time? Then what? How am *I* supposed to get my hands on her if she goes underground?"

"Listen, if you intend to run the business one day, I suggest you figure that out pretty damn quick. Before I ice your dumb ass."

*Ignorant bastard.*

"And Campo? How do you want me to handle him when he shows?"

"Give him and his boys a nice send off after this is over. We might need them to snatch the broad, but I don't like witnesses."

Disgusted, Tony disconnected and tossed the phone, crossed to a table in the corner of the gym, shoved on boxing gloves, and headed for the heavy bag. Pummeling the hell out of it, wishing it was Papa's face, Tony placed several kicks where his groin should be.

*This is my operation and I'll run it my way, old man. Do you think you're Mr. All Powerful, all the way from Vegas? That's a laugh. It's time I made my own mark on the organization. Gained some respect.*

*Where's Ken Davidson, Papa? For all I know, he's already dead in a ditch and you just want to wipe his DNA off the face of the earth by killing his mother and now, his daughter. You've gone completely off your rocker. God, you arrogant prick.*

Tony lashed out with a jab, connecting so hard the bag shuddered. Another jab. A left cross came next and set the chains rattling.

*Who do you think you are? Jesus, you don't have a clue what you're doing.*

An uppercut snapped out, arm bent, fist up. The imagined impact felt terrific, knuckle-crunching awesome. Mind supplying the imagery, Angelo's teeth slammed together and his head snapped back.

*What a laugh.*

Tony paused, chest heaving, then shuffled right, gloves up, guard tight and together.

*Well, I'll show you—just wait. I'll clean up your mess and prove I can run the business—no problem.*

The kick caught the bag mid-swing, stopping it cold.

*Yeah, I'll show you all right. I'm going to be the son you always wanted. Hell, I'll show everyone.*

# Chapter 8

Theo slouched in a chair beside Melena's bed and watched her sleep. She moaned every time she turned over. Those cuts and bruises covering her body were raw and had to sting like the devil. He traced his hand lightly down her arm, hoping to soothe her. She didn't open her eyes. He hoped the pain meds kept her comfortable, but he doubted they would stop the nightmares. He watched her carefully, alert for any signs of the night terrors he knew could follow the attack she had experienced.

Doodlebug slept on a roll-away cot at the end of the bed, a thick swath of bandages protecting his chest where the bullet had been removed. He was out cold, thanks to the tranquilizer Breeana had administered in an I.V. solution. According to Bree, the wolf would be sedated for several hours. It would give his body a better chance to heal from the near-fatal injury. Of course, it was Theo who performed the clean up detail. He had already changed the padding under Dood's body and given him a sponge-bath since laying him on the cot. It was the least he could do, considering the wolf had risked his life to protect Melena.

The house was quiet except for the odd creak of logs settling in the cabin, Dood's heavy breathing, and an argument coming from the next room. Chinked timber walls weren't enough to drown out Sullivan's frustrated baritone. Theo's ears could not help but tune in to the conversation.

"Damn it, Bree. You promised me you'd stay in the boat, and where did you end up? You went crawling through a crime scene to administer CPR to a wolf, for God's sake."

"*I* never said I would stay behind in the boat, Sully. In fact, I never had time to say anything before you charged out of there with Theo."

"That's beside the point. Then just to top it all off, you cut off your cast so you could operate on Dood."

"I did *not* cut off my cast," she huffed. "Effie did it for me. I needed whatever agility I could manage to do the surgery. And Doc made me another one afterward. Did you know Effie was Doc's nurse before she married him?"

"Don't change the damn subject."

There was nothing but silence for long minutes before Theo heard his brother's voice again.

"Hey, it was either kiss you...or strangle you."

*Sully, what are you doing? Here I am babysitting the woman I want to crawl into bed with, and can't, while you're making out with your fiancée in the next room. Have a heart, will ya?*

"Listen, cookie, Campo could have still been out there. What if he had grabbed you? Hurt you?"

"You know...you're right," Breeana said softly. "Maybe you should punish me for disobeying orders."

"You deserve nothing less. Can I use my handcuffs?"

*Oh, for Pete's sake. If this is going to get X-Rated, I'll have to shove in my earplugs. Will you please give me a break?*

"I'll have to think about it." Breeana answered coyly. "You know, I saw Theo rolling Dood down the hallway to Melena's bedroom. He intends to keep an eye on both of them tonight. So, I guess that lets us off the hook." Breeana giggled. "I'll race you to the shower."

"Forget about the shower. Let's share the claw-footed tub. You run the bath and add the bubbles; I'll pour the brandy."

*Jesus, Jesus, Jesus. Make sure you're ready to sleep when you get back to the bedroom, boys and girls, or I'll use my own handcuffs and duct tape to keep things quiet for the rest of the night.*

MELENA OPENED HER EYES, squeezed them shut again and tried once more. He was still there, still sprawled in the chair beside the bed, still watching her. Theo's beard was scruffy, his hair tussled, his jeans split at the knees. His shirt was unbuttoned halfway to his navel revealing a rock-solid chest. He looked dangerous and delicious, sinfully delicious. Morning sun filtered through the skylight and caught the hunger of his gaze. He wanted her. She wanted him. God, she was so stupid.

The last few days had really messed with her head. The men yesterday may not have raped her, but they might as well have. She was damaged in so many ways. She felt dirty because they had touched her. She could still smell Campo on her skin. She needed a bath and a wire brush to scrub herself clean. After that, she wanted to be left alone to cry her heart out.

To rant and rave, and feel sorry for herself. She must be mistaken about the look in Theo's eyes. He couldn't possibly want her, a woman who did not even know her own lineage and was a punching bag for scum. "Go away."

Theo shook his head, his voice rolling over his tongue like sandpaper. "No can do, sugar. Not until I'm sure you can get out of that bed under your own steam."

"Fine." She glared at him, tossed the blankets aside. That was as far as she got. Every muscle seized when she tried to sit up. She clenched her teeth to swallow the sob working its way up her throat and sank back on the pillows. "I'll get up when I want to. Just leave me alone."

Theo uncoiled himself from the chair and loomed over her, offering her a hand. "What's the matter with you? Let me help."

"I don't need your damn help or your pity." Melena covered her face with a pillow. *I don't want you to see me like this. Please, just go home and take everyone else with you.*

"Pity? What the hell are you talking about?" Theo's fists framed her head in the blink of an eye, grabbed the pillow she was hiding behind, and tossed it to the floor. His gaze blazed a trail along her skimpily clad body, the look in his eyes predatory. Nope, there wasn't a drop of pity in sight. "See, I've been watching over you all night, with nothing but time on my hands to fantasize about what it would feel like to do this..."

His mouth captured hers in a molten burst of heat that travelled through her entire length. Surely pity wasn't on the menu if his tongue could plunder her lips to deepen the kiss like that. And there was nothing careful about the way he manhandled her, or shoved her hands aside when she tried to get him to let go. In fact, he pinned her wrists above her head, then nipped his way down her neck to her collarbone, and groaned. Loudly.

Maybe she'd been too hasty in drawing the *pity* conclusion. There was only one way to find out. She writhed beneath him, arching to close the gap with the powerful chest that was mere inches above her own. Her ribs jolted at the movement, stabbing her like a knife where Campo had punched her. *Holy mother of God.* She sucked in a breath as tears filled her eyes.

Theo shot his head up as he brushed a tear from her cheek with the pad of his thumb. "Damn. I hurt you."

"No...n-no...it wasn't you," she managed to say through clenched teeth.

"You'd better be telling me the truth." He held her gaze for another moment before burying his face in her hair. "Hmm, so nice, Mel. I've wanted to taste you all night, and do a hell of a lot more besides. Tell me, would a man who pitied you want to bury himself inside you when you're hurting so badly?"

"That's not fair, Theo. I don't think we can..."

"Now, you might think that I'll do the right thing here; that I'll step away and leave you alone with your misery and pain. But I won't. And if you think for one minute you can lie there in your barely-there sleep shirt and panties feeling sorry for yourself, and I won't take full advantage of the situation, you're dead wrong."

"So, let's get you up and moving toward the bathroom and a hot shower before I change my mind, climb on top of you, and add to your aches and pains with a few more. At least then you'll get the message that I don't *pity* you."

"You bastard."

"You've got that right. But I'll be damned if you'll play the shame game with me. Yesterday happened, sugar. Campo beat the shit out of you. He and his goons had their hands on you. They tried to rape you."

"I know all that. Don't you think I feel bad enough?" Mel pulled another pillow from behind her head and pitched it at his face. "I don't want to talk about it!"

"It wasn't your fault." He caught the pillow and lobbed it on the bed. Scooping her in his arms, he strode out of the room to the bathroom. "As soon as you realize that, you can put it behind you. Campo won't get his hands on you again, that's a promise. So don't let him win by acting like a victim. You're made of stronger stuff than that. And don't turn your back on my help when it's offered, because I can be a son of a bitch, especially when I haven't slept."

Theo set her feet on the bathmat. He kept an arm around her to steady her as he opened the shower door. After turning on the jets, he eased her T-shirt over her head and slid her panties down her legs. It was an impersonal act, one of a friend helping a friend. Then he lifted her over the lip of the shower and closed the door. "I'll be back with a change of clothes and your toothbrush. You need anything else before I get back...holler."

As the hot spray soothed her skin, Melena thought about the man who had just given her back her pride and sanity. Theo Sauvage was a good man, a strong man, a man brave enough to face her fears with her, to help her toss them aside and bury them where they belonged. If only he could help her find out who wanted to hurt her, who may even want her dead.

# Chapter 9

A half hour later, Melena had her the-hell-with-you-and-the-horse-you-rode-in-on attitude back in place. At least she was thinking less like a victim and more like a survivor now. Theo was glad about that. She'd get over this, all right.

He just wasn't sure that *he* would survive. Stripping her naked and putting her in the shower was the hardest thing he'd ever done. Forget about terrorists and bad guys; those were a walk in the park. But Melena naked, well, he'd sure wanted to handle her, too, but it was too soon, and way too fast. So he'd taken a swim instead—about a hundred laps in the bay—before he'd risked seeing her naked again. And that little heart-shaped tattoo on her tush. *Gawd.*

"Are you listening to me? I said I'm not an invalid. And I *am* going to eat breakfast at the table with everyone else. I've got better things to do than lie around here like some swooning female with a case of the vapors."

"You've got nothing to do but get your strength back, sugar. Now that your head is on straight, you don't have to prove anything to anyone, least of all to me. Even a blind man can see you're still in pain. You need to rest, and that's what you're going to do."

"Put a lid on it, Sparky. I'll do what I want, when I want."

Theo knew he was on the losing end of the battle. He raised his hands in defeat and sauntered out the bedroom door. He headed for the kitchen and some sanity. There was no reasoning with Melena once she made up her mind. He couldn't help the grin inching its way across his face. Melena spitting fire was sure better than the woman he'd seen earlier with a broken spirit, feeling worthless and lost.

Cody shot Pierre a sly grin as Theo bellied up to the table and the coffeepot, pouring himself a generous cup. "Hey, Uncle Theo, how come there's trouble in paradise already, when you've only spent one night together?"

"Yeah," Pierre added. "What's up with that?"

Cody snickered before Theo could bang their heads together. "Maybe 'hot lips' could give you some pointers on how to please the lady."

"Boys, that's enough," Breeana chided as she slid heaping plates of bacon, eggs, and toast in front of them. "For your information, Theo did not spend the night with Melena in the biblical sense, not that it's any of your business. He was taking care of her and Doodlebug last night. He slept in a chair."

Cody eyeballed his mother from across the table. "Well, why didn't you and Sully help him then, so he and Melena wouldn't be so snarly this morning?"

"Yeah, bro," Theo said, straddling a chair and pinning Sully in his sights. "Why didn't you and Bree help me out last night? I could have used a few hours of shut-eye."

He watched the color rise from Breeana's neck to her hairline, while his brother glared at him from the opposite end of the table. It was all he could do to keep a straight face.

Sully cleared his throat. "You know the drill when there's trouble brewing. I was awake most of the night performing a combination of...guarding the perimeter and infiltrating defenses."

"That's right," Breeana agreed readily. "And I had a great deal of other...stuff...to do."

"Stuff? Is that so?" Theo queried, his eyebrows raised over the rim of his cup. "What kind of stuff?"

Pierre's gaze met Cody's while Breeana stumbled for words. "Do you have any idea what they're talking about?"

"Get serious." Cody rolled his eyes. "It's easier just to humor them. We'll figure it out later."

Melena chose that moment to ease into the chair beside Cody. She moved with the agility of a ninety-year-old who had just run the Boston marathon. The angry glint in her eyes was hard for Theo to miss. He figured it was her way of telling him to butt out, let her suffer the aches and pains in silence. Maybe no one else would notice. *Roger that.*

She wore black shorts and a tank top Breeana had loaned her. He made a mental note to pick up the rest of her things from her Firebird. She'd been in Chicago for two weeks before arriving at the lake, so she must have some luggage. The teens gawked at her contusions, abrasions, and awkward movements.

"Boys, it's not polite to stare," Breeana admonished.

"I know, Mom," Cody said. "It's just that Mel's really giving you a run for your money. I mean, I think she's got more purple and green splotches than you do."

It was true. Breeana's skin was still marred and discolored from being attacked not so long ago. She started to laugh when she locked gazes with Melena, and they took in the evidence of each other's injuries. The two of them soon dissolved into fits of giggles.

Theo reached for the bacon while quirking an eyebrow in his brother's direction. "I really think they're both insane. They look like a couple of old soldiers just back from the wars...and they're laughing about it."

Melena smiled. "Well, you're a sight for sore eyes yourself, Sparky. You've still got a few bruises, and those stitches over your eyebrow."

"They'll fall out on their own soon enough." Theo was stunned to realize her smile was all it took to light up his world. He didn't have time to dwell on it, though, as the drone of a plane flying low over the house interrupted his thoughts. Everyone looked out the window to catch a glimpse of it through the trees.

"Will you look at that?" Sully moved quickly to the door, across the screened deck, and onto the lawn.

"No kidding." Theo followed him, the others trailing along behind. His gaze locked on the metallic red and white bird soaring overhead. Identifying aircraft was a life-long hobby of his. "That, ladies and gentlemen, is a nineteen-fifty-three DeHavilland DHC-2, Executive Beaver, amphibious seaplane. She's worth a small fortune. I wonder where the heck she hails from?"

"Is she going to land, Uncle Theo?"

"Looks like it, Cody, but she's still too high. She's probably landing much farther up the lake. We get a lot of that here, planes swooping down on the water and taking off again. Usually, it's someone visiting at one of the cottages. Although, this is the first time I've seen that baby. She's a classic and I wouldn't easily forget her."

"Can Pierre and I follow her in the boat?" The boys already thundered for the stairs.

"No way. Keep your distance. You can take Melena's boat out if you want to go for a spin, but I don't want you anywhere near that plane. Are we clear?"

"As crystal. We'll hang with Tara and Mandy for the day and do some windsurfing instead." A few seconds later, the boys whistled for Bear and Bruiser, Cody's dogs, while heading for the boathouse. "Maybe the girls will make us a picnic lunch if we play this right."

Sully placed a hand on Theo's shoulder, edging him down to the swimming dock and away from the women. "What do you think?"

"I think we'd better find out who owns that plane. Whoever it is, the DeHavilland costs major bucks. I don't like strangers on the lake right now, not since Sarah's death and the attacks on Melena."

Sully nodded agreement. "What do you figure? Reinforcements?"

"Maybe." Theo felt the punch of adrenaline invade his bloodstream. "There's only one way to find out. The plane will be easy to spot once it's moored. We'll wait until nightfall and do a meet and greet."

Sully stared at him for a moment, no doubt wondering what he had up his sleeve. Then he cracked a grin. "What about supplies?"

"Not a problem. I have everything we'll need at my place.

"SLOW DOWN. SLOW DOWN!" Theo ripped the throttle from Melena's hand and cut the motor. The bow spewed out of the water, bounced along the dock and crashed against the pier's skirting. "The last thing you need is more bruises. Your landings need major work. Otherwise, you're going to kill yourself."

"At least it was better than the last time," she argued between clenched teeth, using her fists to iron out the kinks in her back as the boat continued to heave up and down in the swells. She let out a shriek with the last roll, slid portside, and pitched toward the edge.

Theo snagged her waistband, pulling her back before she hit the drink. Smooth skin skimmed his fingers under her shorts. She wasn't wearing panties. No, wait...a lacy thong circled low on her hips in a whisper of silk. He removed his hand in a hurry, shoving it in his pocket before Melena caught on to his reconnaissance in her shorts.

The woman was hurting. He had no business thinking about her on anything but professional terms. He might be known for stealth, but what the hell was he doing? *Dumb ass.*

She regained the seat alongside him, wiping water off her sunglasses. "At least I didn't hit the rocks going around the jetty."

"True," he snorted, harnessing his lust. "But that beaver may never recover from the shock of you shaving the fur off the top of his head when you swerved off course."

"Yes!" She cracked a smarmy smile, pumped her fist in the air between them. "Maybe he'll move on then, find someone else's boathouse to build his home in. It took us over an hour this morning to clear out the mess he made in there last night."

Theo dragged his focus away from her water-soaked blouse. Damn, the woman was a wet dream in every sense of the word. The skimpy white cotton molded her breasts, her puckered nipples acting like beacons to a drowning sailor. *Lord in heaven.* "Dood will discourage him, once he's on his feet and in fighting form again."

"Poor Doodlebug," she sighed. "He slept on my bed last night."

Like that was some big, hairy revelation. "I already know, since you insisted I carry him there in the first place. It was an incredible night, sugar. The wolf shares your bed while I sleep in another room. There's something decidedly wrong with that picture."

"Relax, Theo," Melena slid the sunglasses down her nose, her piercing baby-blues nailing him with a glare. "You didn't have a hope in hell of sleeping in my bed anyway. So, tell me, how did Sarah end up with Dood for a pet?"

Theo made the leap from boat to dock, tying off the lines before reaching a hand out to Melena. As her palm slid against his, he said, "She saved his life when he was a pup."

She nodded and he pulled gently, helping her up onto the decking. Tugging on her hand, he settled his arm around her shoulders, anchoring her against his side as they followed the winding path up to the house. The spicy vanilla Melena always wore teased him, hot-wiring his libido, and all bets were off.

His guy parts jumped, muscles cramped, stretched and blistered the front of his cargo shorts with enough heat to topple a redwood. He took stock of the situation while subtly adjusting his zipper.

What exactly had he expected being so close to her? He needed a distraction fast, and the wolf was as good a one as any.

"Sarah drove up here a couple of winters ago to visit Stella. She was out taking a stroll on the ice along the shoreline when she heard an animal scream in the brush. Some poacher had killed a deer, gutted it, and laid traps inside. Dood was so young he didn't sense the danger, the scent of man, and got snared by the neck in a trap. Sarah managed to cut him loose before he choked to death. I guess that's when I understood why she always carried a knife."

"I can't believe anyone could be so cruel, killing a deer, and trying to kill those poor wolves."

"Believe it. It happens all the time. Anyway, it was when Sarah rushed Dood to the vet that she discovered his lineage. Dood's a hybrid—part malamute. It explained why he was shunned by the pack, off hunting on his own. Dood is much bigger than the average male wolf. I don't imagine the Alpha of the pack wanted him hanging around once he'd started a growth spurt."

"But, what about now? Does Dood stay up here alone all winter?"

"No, he has a home with you, if you want him. Sarah bought a ten-acre estate in Rigaud, in the boonies of Montreal. The estate belongs to you now. The perimeter is fenced. The gates are electronic, to keep Dood in and strangers out."

"Just remember, Dood will always be half-wild and needs his freedom. As long as you respect that, you won't have any problems with him. But, if he's going to complicate your life, I'll be happy to keep him with me. I can easily move to a more suitable location and commute to my office in Montreal."

*Of course, it would be terrific if the two of us could move in together.* Get real. He didn't know Melena, shouldn't entertain wild fantasies about sleeping with her, not to mention the other, much deeper connections his soul seemed to attach to this woman.

The timing sucked. She had emerged as the victim here. He sensed she was in extreme danger, just as Sarah had been. And Sarah was already dead.

Was this the legacy of the will? Did someone—some distant relative he wasn't aware of—benefit from the estate if Melena suffered a similar fate to her grandmother's? He needed to find out and keep a clear head while he did. His big head needed to stay on top of the situation, not the little head in his pants begging for action.

"There's no need, Theo. Dood and I will get along fine. I plan to find him a pretty malamute puppy to keep him company."

He laughed. "Good luck with that. He's not neutered. You'll frustrate the hell out of him." *Like you're doing to me, and Dood and I aren't ready for the chop shop.*

He could see the wheels turning inside Melena's head, her face a study of concentration. "What about an older female then, one that's already neutered?"

Besides her sex appeal, the woman had an impressive brain. "You know, that just might work."

"I hadn't realized Sarah had an estate in Rigaud. Maybe I should sit down and actually read the will."

"Couldn't hurt," he said. "Why don't we go over it in a few days, after things settle down?"

# Chapter 10

Cody flew up the stairs onto Melena's deck as Theo fired up the barbeque. "Hey. How was your day with the girls, champ?"

"Great, Uncle Theo." Cody had that guilty look, a question forming on his tongue. "Listen, do you mind setting another place for dinner?"

"No problem, big guy." He nudged the peak of the kid's baseball cap. "Just tell me her name, so I don't make a mistake with the introductions."

"It's not a her...it's a him. I brought back Mr. DeHavilland for dinner. Actually, his name isn't DeHavilland. It's Tom Sawyer, like in the Mark Twain books. He's down tying up his boat with Pierre."

"What? I told you to stay clear of that plane."

"I know, but it was a total accident. I bumped into him, you know? Besides, he's a really nice guy. He's rented a cottage near the dam and hasn't had time to buy groceries yet. I figured you'd want to meet him, find out more about his plane, so I invited him to chow down with us."

"You figured right, but that doesn't let you and Pierre off the hook. The boats are off limits to both of you until I say different."

"Ah, come on, Uncle Theo. I know I screwed up, but...would you change your mind if we split some wood and mowed the grass for Melena?"

"Don't count on it. No privileges if you can't toe the line. You guys can start by setting the table for dinner. Get Pierre up here to help you."

Theo watched him go. Cody was right about one thing; he was interested in *anyone* who showed up uninvited since Mel's attack, especially Mr. DeHavilland.

The guy buzzed the cottage while making his descent on the lake this morning, as if he knew the place. He also had big bucks to throw around, if the plane was any indication. The kind of money that could pay for hired muscle.

Sully came out of the house and shut the door. "I heard you talking to Cody. Who is this guy and what does he want?"

"There's only one way to find out. Let's go welcome our guest. He might enjoy a cold beer."

Sully laughed.

MELENA, BREEANA AND the boys carried the steaks, veggie pack and other food prepped for the barbeque outside to the deck. That's when she realized she had a visitor, someone she didn't know. Possibly one of her neighbors calling to introduce himself? She watched as Theo and Sully sauntered up the stairs with an older man, mid forties and physically fit, his skin sun-weathered as if he spent a lot of time outdoors.

It wasn't Theo's casual body language that first set off the alarm bells inside her head. It was the predatory gleam of his eyes. He tracked the man's progress as if he waited for an excuse to kill him.

The stranger didn't pay much attention. He stood at the top of the steps, his gaze riveted to her. She saw recognition in his eyes, but that made no sense at all. How could he know her when she'd never laid eyes on him?

What happened next really scared the pants off her. Without warning, Theo plastered the man face down on the deck, shoved a knee into his back, wrenched a gun from the waistband beneath the man's shirt, and pressed it against his skull. Then he hollered to Cody and

Pierre to take her and Breeana back in the cabin. Breeana allowed the boys to steer her inside, no doubt more for their protection than hers.

Theo swore when *she* refused to move and stood rooted to the deck. "Mel, get in the damn house."

"No, I'm not budging, not when this involves me. I'm sick and tired of men coming at me with guns and their fists. Who is this creep?"

"He says his name is Tom Sawyer. He flew in on that plane today."

She watched Sully's hands move with precision down Sawyer's legs while Theo held him down. "He's clean, bro. You can let him up."

In an instant, Theo dragged the man to his feet and threw him against the side of the house. He spun him around and pressed his forearm against the man's larynx, fitting the gun snuggly beneath Sawyer's upturned chin. Melena held her breath, praying the gun didn't go off.

"Who the hell are you?" Theo hissed, pushing hard against Sawyer. "Who sent you here?"

She touched Theo's shoulder, her hand shaking. "Let him go. This isn't Campo."

Ignoring her, he passed the gun over to Sully, grip first, and eased his hold on Sawyer so the man could get a word out without choking on it. Theo swept her behind him with his other arm and pinned her there. "I'm not a patient man, Sawyer. Start talking."

"Take it easy, will you?" Sawyer cleared his throat and made eye contact, his gaze steady, his breathing even for a man in his position. "As I've already told Cody, my name is Tom Sawyer and I'm a businessman from Anchorage. I'm here on vacation, just passing through really. I rented a cottage on Silver Lake for a few days, and then I'm headed for Las Vegas."

Sully leafed through Sawyer's wallet. "His ID matches what he's saying. There's an Anchorage address on the driver's license, and a confirmation number for a hotel reservation in Las Vegas. The check-in date is three days from now."

Theo didn't seem convinced and she understood why. Sawyer carried a concealed weapon, for Pete's sake. And the timing was too perfect. Someone hunted her, intended to do her physical harm, and this man meandered into the picture by coincidence?

Theo grabbed Sawyer by the collar, shoved him into a chair while maintaining a protective arm around her waist. "Why did you choose Silver Lake? Why rent a cottage here?"

Sawyer wiped the salt from his upper lip and mopped his sweaty brow with the back of an arm. He might not know how high the stakes were, but he didn't appear to be a complete fool. The guy had good reason to be nervous.

"This isn't the first time I've stopped at Silver Lake. It's a hell of a long flight from Alaska to Vegas. I often take a few days here to unwind. Look, check at the store with Stella if you don't believe me. She's rented me the cabin before."

Melena supposed it was possible. She was sure Theo would talk to Stella to be sure. He said he'd never seen the man's plane before it flew overhead this morning.

"Do you always fly the DeHavilland?" she asked.

Sawyer shook his head and looked straight at her. "Nope, she's a new acquisition. I wanted to test her out thoroughly. That's why I decided on such a long flight. I've had to puddle jump along the way, of course. But, she's definitely airworthy and hasn't let me down."

Theo frowned at his brother. "Is there a permit in Sawyer's wallet for carrying concealed?"

Sully rechecked the wallet's contents. "Can't say that there is, bro. No Canadian firearms permit at all, although he's licensed to carry concealed in his home state."

"Look, I realize how bad this looks." Sawyer said, shifting uncomfortably in the chair. "The truth is I often carry large sums of money with me on these trips, when I'm planning to gamble." He managed a forced laugh. "I'm also in the habit of carrying protection, although I know I shouldn't carry a weapon in Canada. I didn't want to leave my Sig on the plane or in the cabin in case someone broke in. I apologize for scaring you folks out of your wits."

"I want to see the color of the money you're so busy protecting, Sawyer." Theo hauled him out of the chair and gave him a shove. "It's not in your pockets, so where is it?"

"In my backpack, under the bow of the boat," he offered by way of explanation. "I thought it would be safer there than in the cabin."

Tipping his chin at his brother, Theo said, "Let's see what you find."

Sully returned a few minutes later after checking out Sawyer's story. He carried a backpack. "Looks like he's telling the truth. There's at least fifty thousand here."

Theo eyed Sawyer for a long moment, tossed the backpack into his arms, and lowered his guard a fraction. "Don't show up here with a weapon again, Mr. Sawyer. Not if you expect to live and tell about it. You'll get the Sig back when you're ready to leave. Meanwhile, you're welcome to join us for dinner."

Melena thought anyone in their right mind would have cut loose and run, trailing the bag of loot behind them while they still had the chance. But, Tom Sawyer obviously didn't have both oars in the water, because he still wanted to join her happy gang for dinner and some more fun and frolic.

Theo was right, the man bore careful watching. He was either an idiot...or a nerves-of-steel killer. The problem was Theo still didn't seem sure which category he belonged in.

He held her back when she would have followed Sawyer inside the house. Residual adrenaline flooded her system. And it didn't take a crystal ball to know Theo was furious she hadn't run for cover with the boys and Breeana when he'd told her to. "You scare the hell out of me. When I tell you to move—you move."

She struggled to shrug out of his grip. "I'm not one of your soldiers, Sparky. I sure don't take orders from you. So, don't expect me to dance to your tune." She rammed a finger into his chest for emphasis. "This is about me. I have every right to be here. Besides, didn't I tell you he wasn't Campo?"

"How do you know he wasn't a threat, even if he wasn't Campo?" Theo snapped. He hauled her up in his arms an inch from his face. His gaze dropped to her lips. His head lowered to a hairsbreadth away from her mouth. She knew he was right, but stubbornness wouldn't allow her to admit it.

"You are so incredibly naïve. Don't you realize Sawyer could have hired Campo to come after you? Hell, he could be the brains behind this whole vendetta against you. He could also be the one who had Sarah murdered. That bag of money could be to pay off his thugs. Whether you like it or not, I intend to protect you. And I don't care if you agree with my tactics or not."

Melena's body tightened when his lips crashed down on hers, her response involuntary. She wrapped her arms around his neck and held on, her Nikes dangling a foot off the ground. His taste roared through her while his woodsy scent enveloped her, sent her spiraling out of control. The fit was right, her body's response so wanton, so much more than the last time his mouth closed over hers when she was flat on her back in bed this morning. That experience had only hinted at the secrets of this man.

She wanted him beyond reason. Her senses reeled at his taste, his texture. The press of his body against hers only made her want him more. She needed his skin against hers, his heat driving into her. He plunged deeper into her mouth and raked his teeth over her tongue while she burned out of control.

"Hey! I thought 'hot lips' held first prize in the lip sucking department." At the sound of that voice, their heads shot up to see Cody gaping at them through the screen door. "Jeez, Uncle Theo, you should rent a room."

"Get lost, kid."

"Well, that was embarrassing." Melena managed to squeak.

Theo laughed, touching his forehead to hers as she fought to even her breathing. Thank God they hadn't stripped each other naked before the teen appeared on the scene. They'd both lost control at the touch of their lips. She sighed with regret, guessing he wouldn't lose focus again, not as long as someone was after her. He bent and brushed a final kiss across her mouth. Then he opened the door and nudged her inside ahead of him.

That's when they came face to face with another pair of eyes—eyes that glared at Theo as if they wanted him dead. Tom Sawyer drilled him with a stare that could melt polar ice.

Melena felt the primal urge to wipe the floor with Sawyer for staring at Theo that way. She shook her head and almost laughed at the absurdity of the situation. The idea of the brawny warrior behind her needing protection from her was ridiculous. Still, her challenging glare at Sawyer seemed to do the trick. Sensing her disapproval, he reversed direction and strode deeper inside the cabin.

The rest of the evening was a complete disaster. It was painfully obvious Theo didn't trust Sawyer. Although his expression remained stoic at the dinner table, his body language spoke volumes. He wanted Sawyer gone. The look on his face clearly said *"Here's your hat. What's your hurry?"* as he watched and waited to attack the man at the least provocation.

Sawyer hardly dared glance across the table at anyone, especially her. Every time he did, Theo picked up on it and stared him down. The only saving grace during the entire fiasco was the boys. If the teens noticed the undercurrents playing the room, they didn't let on. Trust kids to keep a conversation going about anything and everything, everything except the elephant in the room.

Sighing heavily a short time later, Sawyer reclaimed his gun from Theo, said a polite "goodbye" to her and trudged down to the pier...with Theo running up the backs of his heels. Sawyer started the motor, swung his runabout away from the dock, and hit the running lights, heading into the darkness.

The signs were as clear as the stars blazing the night sky. Theo would never allow Sawyer to get close to her again, whether he was a threat or not. There would be no casual nuances of friendship, no dropping by for a cup of coffee, or to shoot the breeze.

Theo stood on the dock in front of her and watched Sawyer's boat until it disappeared around a bend of shoreline. Sawyer was the last to leave. Sully and Breeana had already corralled the boys, the dogs, and returned to Theo's house a few kilometers up the lake.

Melena inhaled deeply, savoring the night breeze scented with pine, and Theo. She'd gotten too close to him. They hadn't even made love, yet his essence branded her like a permanent scar. It served her right for letting him kiss her.

She would know him anywhere now, be able to pick him out of a crowd the length of a football field. The angle of his jaw, those mysterious coffee-colored eyes, and the feel of his strong body all etched in her brain, into her heart, a heart yearning to be part of him in more than the physical sense.

She knew that wouldn't happen. Theo was a warrior. He belonged to that breed of men who avoided serious relationships at all costs.

As if reading her thoughts, he glanced at her over his shoulder. "Get your purse and lock up, sugar. We're heading out."

They clowned in the Firebird like a couple of teenagers with Theo behind the wheel. It wasn't long before they pulled into the parking lot of a local watering hole. Melena could see rows of vehicles surrounding the long wooden building. Neon signs flashed beer slogans across the hoods of cars and trucks nearest the windows.

*Charlie's* was a converted barn that was sectioned into dining and dance areas. Decorated with country flair, wagon wheels chained to the ceiling and strung with fairy lights illuminated the structure. An old sleigh occupied a corner of the dining room, doubling as a salad bar.

Antique firearms, kerosene lamps and farm tools decorated the walls. Red-checked tablecloths topped with white candles adorned the round tables.

By the time Theo ordered their drinks, the band was tuned up and requesting all line-dancers to get out on the floor. He was quick to comply.

"Come on, city girl," he teased, pulling her to her feet to join him.

"I *can't* go out there. I've never line-danced in my life."

He chuckled at the obvious panic in her eyes. "Well, there's no time like the present to get started. I guess I forgot to tell you, I'm a dancing fool."

He planted a kiss on her temple and dragged her by the hand onto the dance floor, all the while ignoring her pleas to return to the table.

"Well heck, that's just terrific. And me with my two left feet," she grumbled, blowing the hair out of her eyes. "You sure picked a fine time to tell me this, Mr.-Dancing-With-The-Stars."

He grinned, his dark eyes flashing in amusement as his eyebrows waggled. "Sorry it never came up before. It's okay, sugar. It's simple, really. I lead and you follow. Now, this one's the Continental."

He moulded her to his side until she understood the steps involved. Within a few minutes, she hooted and stomped like a real pro, except for heading in the wrong direction on the quarter turns. Theo flanked her every move and swung her about each time she turned in the wrong direction. The next ninety minutes passed by in a blur of laughter and her clumsy dance moves. She couldn't remember when she'd had so much fun. Or felt so jealous.

Women ogled Theo like he was eye candy. Well, he was. But he was *her* eye candy, at least for tonight. The blue jeans he wore hugged his thighs and butt in all the right places. A crisp white shirt offset smooth tanned skin, mile-wide shoulders and heavily muscled arms. He smelled like soap, the outdoors, and musky male. When he smiled that rakish grin of his, her heart beat double-time. Then it crashed to a mind-numbing halt.

Realization dawned with thundering clarity. Theo had spoiled her for ever wanting another man. Studying the angles of his face and play of muscles rippling his torso, Melena knew she had already lost the battle. Her heart belonged to him now. She had fallen hard and fast for the one man she shouldn't have. *Crap.*

What was she thinking? Where was her common sense? Her mind understood Theo was a warrior, a fighter who would right the wrongs of the world wherever he could. Her soul insisted from the beginning that she stay away from him. He was a lone wolf, after all. An alpha male destined to walk his path in life alone.

His allegiance to her only stemmed from his obligations to her grandmother. He would fulfill those obligations, she was sure, and make tracks for the nearest exit at the first opportunity.

But, her betraying body argued he would also be a magnificent lover if he stuck around. If that melt-your-socks kiss this afternoon was anything to go by. Still, sex with Theo would be a memory almost before it began. He wouldn't wait around to warm her bed in the morning. He'd be long gone before her eyes even opened. And he'd break her heart into a million pieces.

Mental health alert—she could enjoy their time together and draw the line at anything more intimate. Sure, she could. *Well, can't I?*

The song ended and Theo tightened his hold, his chin resting against the top of her head. Feeling confused, Melena tried to put some distance between them as she struggled to get the words out. "Whew. You tired me out. I have to make a pit stop before we head back to the lake."

He swept her up in his arms again and pivoted her backward, lightly nuzzling her neck. "Okay, sugar. I'll dance you over to the door marked *Cowgirls* and wait for you in the hallway."

Melena's breath hitched as her body's reaction to Theo edged into the *I'm on fire* zone. Too soon, it was over—or maybe not soon enough for her confused state of mind. "Thanks. I won't be long."

# Chapter 11

Theo loved watching Melena learn the various dance moves. Laughter shone in the cobalt-blue of her eyes. Her hair framed her face like pixie fire when he swung her in his arms under the overhead lights. A sultry pout graced her lips each time she focused on a new dance step, shaking that little jean-clad tush of hers to the music. The ivory silk of her blouse clung to the shape of her breasts and left enough exposed cleavage to make him growl.

He knew other men watched her. She was poetry in motion, like the old song. But she was all his, until the danger was over. Then she could pick up the remnants of her life and dance with whomever she wanted.

But, not tonight, and pity the poor bastard who thought differently. He wouldn't allow any man to cut in on them on the dance floor, although several had been stupid enough to try. He didn't know where the danger to Melena lay, but he sensed it was here. Like a crouching tiger waiting to pounce. He was ready, his back-up piece strapped to his ankle. His body and mind prepped for violence.

He waited outside the bathroom for Melena, his eyes searching the crowd. And couldn't believe who strolled out of the men's room and slammed into him.

THE RESTROOM WAS DESERTED since the band had announced the last song for the evening, a waltz. Although Melena had danced most of the night, she knew she was tipsy. She wasn't a big drinker or a big woman. It took very little alcohol to have this warm, fuzzy effect.

She stopped at a sink to run cold water into her hands then splash it on her face, grabbing paper towels from the dispenser to dry herself off. A breeze from an open window cooled her overheated skin.

As the first strains of Shania Twain filled the room, Melena made eye contact in the mirror with a heavyset woman who had entered the bathroom and smiled into eyes hidden behind oversized pop-bottle glasses. There was something oddly familiar about her.

Maybe they'd crossed paths earlier on the dance floor. Maybe she was one of those women perusing Theo as if he was a late night snack. Melena nodded politely and entered a stall before the song ended and the bathroom filled with the departing crowd.

A knife swung through the opening as she turned to close the door. It grazed her shoulder with a sting of pain. Adrenaline kicked like a mule, gave her the strength she needed to slam the door and slide the bolt in place. Scrambling on top of the toilet lid, she scrunched down to avoid the arc of blade slashing over and under the door with quick bursts. She screamed at the top of her lungs.

The music was too loud. Theo would never hear her.

She tugged her cell phone out of her jean's pocket with sweaty hands. It flew from her fingers, slid to the floor, and out of the stall.

Blood trickled down her sleeve and Melena looked around frantically. She needed a weapon.

Her eyes landed on the ceramic tank lid on the back of the toilet. Pulling it free and clutching it in both hands, she threw back the latch on the door and charged through.

Too late, a whisper of movement fanned her cheek. Knife Woman hadn't gone far. She knocked the tank lid out of Melena's hands with a swipe of a well muscled arm, dragged Melena to the window, and launched her through the opening like a human cannonball.

Melena landed on a shoulder and rolled while gasping for breath. Her attacker hadn't cleared the window yet. There was enough ballast on the big-boned woman to make it a tight squeeze. She staggered to her feet and, weaving like a drunk through a back alley, headed for the parking lot and *Charlie's* front door.

She had to hurry. She was almost there.

Someone seized her by the arm and spun her around. Six feet of hatred pulled her toward him—*Campo*—his eyes were dark holes of mean. Melena screamed and fought like a banshee.

"Settle down." Campo squeezed her neck to make his point. She bit back a whimper, blinking away tears until her vision cleared. Shoving her in front of him, he headed for the road, stopping only to cock his head at the woman who was down on all fours under the window. "Get your lard ass over here and give me a hand with the package."

"I lost the knife, man," she said.

"Forget about the frigging knife. You're wearing gloves so there's no chance of prints. Move your butt or I'll leave you here for the pigs."

Nausea flooded Melena's stomach. Bile crept up her throat. She clamped a hand over her mouth. She could throw up later when she had time. Right now she had more pressing matters to deal with, such as her life or death. These freaks had been hired to deliver her to someone. *Oh, God!*

An SUV idled nearby on the road, a guaranteed one-way trip to hell if she got inside that vehicle. Theo would never find her then.

Flanked by Campo and the woman, Melena kicked and screamed as they dragged her toward the vehicle's open door. Fear squeezed her heart like a vice. She tamped it down and cleared her head.

The parking lot was deserted; "last call" from the bar had given patrons the chance to order more drinks for the road. Surely someone would hear her screams and come to her rescue.

*Where is Theo? Doesn't he realize I am in trouble?*

In her periphery, she saw a man streak between two parked cars and leap onto the hood of a third. He jackknifed off a pick-up, flew through the air, and brought them all down with a grinding crunch. Melena lay on the ground beneath Tom Sawyer's body, the air sucked from her lungs. Her shoulder ached. Someone was moaning. Was that her making those terrible noises? Her abductors tried to kick Sawyer off her. He absorbed the punts and refused to budge.

"You're okay, baby. You're okay." Sawyer raised his head enough to glance at her face as he grimaced with pain. "I won't let them take you."

Melena stared into his eyes as he said the words. His expression suggested she was someone important to him. That didn't make any sense at all.

A flash of movement caught her eye over his shoulder. Campo had a gun aimed at Sawyer's head. Before she could scream out a warning, Theo charged out of the darkness. He fired off a shot and Campo spun, clutching his wrist as his weapon hit the ground. Realizing he was outgunned, he raced for the road like a stampeding elephant. The woman pounded the pavement close behind him.

"Stay down!" Theo shouted as he hurtled after them, zigzagging as he fired off a couple more rounds. Her attackers reached the SUV and dove inside. A second later, the vehicle peeled rubber on asphalt, an explosion of gunfire flashing from its windows.

In a hail of bullets, Theo hit the pavement between two cars and didn't move.

TONY PEERED THROUGH the windshield as the SUV swerved around an S-curve. The old logging road was a narrow break in the trees up ahead. "Don't miss the turn off."

"I see it." Frankie hit the brakes and skidded to the right, spinning the steering wheel in the opposite direction to keep the truck on the road and out of an approaching ditch.

"Goddamn you're stupid." Campo sneered at Tony from the backseat. He sat beside Rico, wrapping a handkerchief around his nicked wrist. "We don't need to dick around on back country roads when there's no one following us for miles. Turn this thing around and head for the lodge. I need a first aid kit."

Ignoring him, Tony motioned for Frankie to continue along the dirt road.

"Did you hear me?" Campo roared. "Where the hell are we going?"

Branches scraped along the running boards as they bumped over rutted tire tracks nosing deeper into the forest. "We're switching rides. The cops will be searching for this one in no time flat."

"Okay, so you're not as dumb as you look," Campo mocked. "Still, you're a sorry-assed excuse for a Don's kid. You really think you've got the balls to follow in Daddy's footsteps?"

Tony shot him a glare. "I've got balls enough."

"Oh, yeah?" Campo laughed. "Then why don't you show them? To hear Angelo tell it, you're only along on this gig to puke your guts out when things get messy. He knows you'll never measure up."

"We'll have to wait and see, won't we? Who knows, maybe the old man's got a thing or two to learn himself."

"That's crazy talk." Campo reached forward, pinched Tony's shoulder until it hurt. "Vincelli won't take shit from the likes of you, even if you are his kid. If you know what's good for you, you'll follow my lead. Keep your trap shut and obey orders, or he might ask me to toughen you up."

Tony said nothing, laughing inwardly in response.

The road ended at a turnaround a few minutes later and they pulled off into a thicket of conifers. Frankie shoved the SUV into park and everyone got out. A half-moon shone overhead, bright enough to see Silver Lake sparkling through a windbreak in the distance.

A loon called to its mate with a mournful warble. The rustle of leaves on the forest floor warned night creatures were on the move...some big, some small...the hunters and the hunted.

"This place gives me the creeps," Campo said. "Give me the nightlife in a big city any day of the week." His gaze swept the shadows before he turned back to Tony. "Where's the other wheels? I don't see them. You screw up again?"

Tony palmed the .22 revolver and pointed it at Campo's head. Frankie reacted instantly, grabbed Campo from behind while Rico frisked him for the weapons he carried—his ankle piece and a knife.

"Not this time, Campo. If you'd been nicer to me, it might have made a difference. But you're a miserable prick and you messed up with Salera. Three times. This is the end of the road for you."

"Very funny. For Christ's sake, Tony, cut the B.S. I'm getting pissed now. And if I get pissed enough, I'll tell your old man what a pathetic loser you are."

"That'd be an interesting conversation. Unfortunately, you don't have time to make the call. By the way—Angelo sends his regards."

Tony fired twice, tapped Campo in the forehead and again in the heart. The look of surprise in Campo's dead eyes made it worthwhile. "You weren't expecting it, were you, asshole?"

"Nice work, boss," Rico said, clearly stunned at what had gone down. The underlying respect in his voice gave Tony confidence.

"Pick up this sack of shit and toss him in the lake."

Frankie and Rico headed for the water dragging Campo's dead body between them. Tony climbed back into the SUV.

*Son of a bitch. Melena Salera slipped through our fingers tonight because of her old man. Ken Davidson sprawled on top of her so we couldn't haul her out of there. Christ. It was him, all right. He's hardly changed in all these years. Guess that's what honest living does for a man.*

*What do I do? No one else knew Ken in the old days, didn't recognize him tonight, so the news is mine to tell. I need a plan...Papa's bound to go apeshit. Should I give him a double header? Two for the price of one?*

*Why the hell not? I'll offer him Melena and Ken together. That'll get him to Silver Lake in a hurry. Then he'll see for himself that I'm in control.*

*First, I have to find them, but that's almost a done deal. One call to Melena's cell phone and she'll trip all over herself to come to me. After I threaten to blow Theo Sauvage's head off and kill every member of his family.*

*Yeah, it'll work. She's in love with the crazy bastard. She'll protect him. I could see it in her eyes when they were on the dance floor tonight.*

*When I have her, her old man will follow suit without lifting a finger to protect himself. Because Daddy loves his little girl—enough to die for her.*

Tony chuckled, absently noticed the stain on a cuff and stripped off the shirt. No point in arriving at the lodge spattered in brain matter.

# Chapter 12

"It's only a scratch. See? Just five stitches to close the wound. I'm fine, Theo."

Melena's face was white, but the stubborn tilt of her bruised chin was evident. Theo ran a finger along her jaw, smoothed the tape closing a gash under her chin, and breathed a shaky sigh of relief.

He'd been acting like a madman out in the waiting room. Sawyer had held him back to give hospital staff a chance to tend Melena's injuries. The nurses had repeatedly assured him the wound to her shoulder was superficial, that there was no arterial damage. Still, he'd needed to see for himself.

"Yeah, by some miracle it wasn't life threatening. Certainly, no thanks to me."

She glared at him as she struggled to sit up on the gurney. "What else were you supposed to do to protect me? Go with me into the ladies room?"

"Damn straight. I was supposed to be doing my job, not lounging around in a hallway while you were being attacked."

"Is that all I am to you? *A job?* Is that what you care about? Your male ego is deflated because you didn't ride to the rescue the second I was attacked?"

He braced an arm around her, helped her get her legs over the side to slide off the gurney. "You're an itch I can't scratch, sugar, so you'd better get used to it. And yeah, for some reason I have these finely tuned protective urges where you're concerned."

Easing off her bloody blouse, he pulled off his own shirt and buttoned Melena into it. "Look, if anyone else had been assaulted tonight I wouldn't feel like such an ass. People get hurt all the time, and I'm only one man. That's a fact. But it's *you* who was knifed tonight. I can't get around that. No way. No how. And I promise you—no one's getting a chance at you again. They'll have to come through me first."

A shimmer of tears in her eyes, Melena came into his arms and rested her head over his pounding heart. *Damn.* He had to keep his distance from her, although God only knew how he would manage it. The woman blindsided him with feelings he didn't want to pin a label on. "Let's get you home."

Sawyer waited outside the door to the examining room. He was bent at the waist with his hands on his knees. He straightened as soon as the door opened. If he suffered any residual aches and pains of his own, he didn't let on. Instead, he flanked Melena on the opposite side to Theo. They walked down the hallway and outside to the Firebird and Sawyer's borrowed van, keeping a wary eye on their surroundings. Sawyer lightly embraced Melena and gave her a peck on the cheek.

"Thank you," Melena said to him. "Thanks for helping me tonight."

Sawyer didn't say a word.

Theo helped her into the vehicle and secured her seatbelt. He rounded the car to the driver's side, opened the door, and held Tom's gaze. "I owe you."

"Forget about it." Sawyer scribbled something on a scrap of paper and shoved it at him. "Call if you need me. Anytime...day or night. That's one special woman you've got there. Keep her safe and be careful, man. There were at least three goons in that SUV and they all acted like pros."

"You're right." *And how would you know they were pros, Sawyer?* Theo's blood boiled at the thought. He forced himself to relax. "It looks like we've got ourselves a tag team."

"You'll catch them, man; I know you will. I'm here if you want my help."

"I appreciate it." Theo's gaze locked on the older man's with unease. Tom Sawyer was a complete stranger, only staying at the lake for a few days. Yet, he wanted to help Melena. Why? His best guess was that Sawyer was somehow involved. His little voice insisted he needed to solve the riddle of Tom Sawyer while he had the chance. Before it was too late.

MELENA COULDN'T CALM down when she got back to the cottage. Although Theo insisted, she refused to take the pain medication prescribed by the doctor. It would knock her for a loop. She couldn't lose a grip on whatever sanity she had left. Her bravado spreading thin, she needed to keep busy. She moved to the kitchen and pulled the bread knife from its wooden block.

"What are you doing?"

Knife in hand, she searched the cupboards, came up with a frying pan and banged it on the stove. She opened the fridge next and stuck her head inside. "What does it look like I'm doing? I'm cooking. I thought sausages and French toast would be good."

"You want breakfast at three in the morning?" Theo eyed her when she hauled the eggs, sausages and bread out of the fridge. He pulled a T-shirt on over his head, grabbed the knife from her grasp, then dragged her away from the stove. Amusement softened the corners of his mouth.

"Sugar, you're on edge. This isn't the time for you to be playing with knives or using hot appliances. Besides, if you eat right now, you'll pop your cookies."

He turned her out of the kitchen and hustled her onto the screened deck. "Take a seat and relax while I brew a pot of tea."

"Brew some *tea*?" she said. "My life is in the toilet and you want me to drink tea? No, get me a double scotch on the rocks, at least."

"No can do." He shook his head, draped an arm around her, and planted a kiss below her ear. "How about taking your pain meds?"

"No pain meds. No tea," she insisted, slinking out from under his arm. "I want a double scotch rocks."

He squeezed her nape, when she would have headed for the bar, and reeled her back. His mouth slid over hers, teasing her with his taste, but not giving her what she wanted.

She needed swinging-from-the-chandelier-gorilla-sex. But the kiss was designed to scramble her brain and make her forget about the scotch. There was nothing worse than a placating kiss when she was in the mood for hot, dark and steamy, something to make her forget the cesspool of her existence. She let out a growl of exasperation.

Rather than argue the merits of that simmering kiss, she turned her back and stormed off to pace the hallway of the cabin. Before long Theo blocked her path. He steered her toward the bedroom with confident strides. *Ah-ha.* Maybe a sexual explosion was in the works, after all.

"Get out of your clothes while I run you a bath. You're wearing holes in the floor."

A bath by herself wasn't quite what she had hoped for. Melena whirled and punched him square in the arm. "I don't want a bath. I don't want to be patronized. And I don't want to be patted on the head and sent to my room like a child!"

He bunched the front of her shirt, holding her to him as he unbuttoned his way between her breasts and down the sensitive skin of her belly. Her jeans unsnapped in a heated movement that scorched her abdomen beneath his fingers.

Even so, he didn't want her. His touch was as benign as the doctor's in the ER. "Easy. I'm trying to give you a hand here. It might help if you'd tell me what you *do* want, besides the scotch."

*I want to forget my life. I want you to surround me with mind-numbing sex.* She cocked a hip, her hands tightening into fists holding the edges of the shirt closed against her chest. Pain and exhaustion tightened her features until she thought her face might disintegrate.

"What I *want* is action. What I *need* is to step up the pace on digging into my past. Someone is out to get me. Meanwhile, we sit by waiting for the next attack and drinking *tea*. I'm so damn sick of it!"

"I'm already on top of it." He banded an arm around her waist and dragged her further into the bedroom. "Your adoption records will arrive by special messenger tomorrow."

What Theo didn't say was they didn't expect to find out much from those documents. No clues in flashing neon as to why someone had murdered her grandmother and wanted her out of commission, as well. The best case scenario? They would find her biological mother and maybe she had a story to tell. But, it was going to be damn painful for her to meet with the woman who had tossed her aside.

Theo's gaze travelled the length of her body. "Take off your clothes or I'll do it for you."

"Is this your idea of foreplay?" she countered.

"Sugar, you'll know when it's foreplay," he said, raising an eyebrow. "You won't have to ask."

When she started to move, he smirked and was gone. Although far from mollified, Melena sank into the claw-footed tub a few minutes later.

Lavender-scented bubbles enveloped her as she relaxed. She stretched the length of the tub and acknowledged that Theo had been right. A hot bath was what she needed to calm the panic sloshing in the pit of her stomach. Unbelievably, she soon drifted off to sleep and dreamed of Theo. He made searing love to her in the dream. Her body heat rose, reacting to his imaginary touch.

# Chapter 13

Theo hauled himself out of the lake and onto the dock in one fluid motion. Not wanting to leave Melena alone, he hadn't stayed in long. Just long enough to wash away the strain of the day and ease the perpetual hard-on that pounded with zeal between his legs.

Doing the right thing was costing him—big time. It made him short-tempered, but there was little he could do about it. Hell, she was his client, not his lover. He shouldn't have to remind himself of that. Still, there was no denying he wanted her.

He air-dried on his way up from the dock, stepping back into his shorts before slipping through the screen door to the kitchen. The house was quiet. Too quiet. He checked her bedroom. No Melena. He moved on to the bathroom, knocking softly at the door. No answer. He pushed inside, and there she was. Every glorious inch of her sound asleep in the bathtub.

A sensuous smile curved her lips, one small hand draped in slumber across the perfect swell of her breasts, their rose-petal peaks budding above the water. She sighed, her knees softly parting, allowing him full view of the silky triangle between her thighs.

His erection whipped to attention while he longed to fall between those creamy thighs, to push her knees still farther apart, to lower his head and sip his fill of her. He wanted to discover her most intimate secrets. To drive her, heat her until the air filled with her scent. Until she couldn't hold back from his teasing caresses. Then he wanted to push them both over the edge.

*Hell no.* That wasn't going to happen.

Theo crossed to the tub and pulled the plug, determined not to weaken at the open invitation displayed by her body. She had sunk so low in the bath that the shoulder bandage leached water, a risk for possible infection.

He focused on that instead of the pulsing surge of his crotch. Once the tub drained, he scooped her into his arms and moved swiftly along the hallway that led to her bedroom. He would dry her, cover her and get the hell away from her.

As he blotted her skin with a fluffy white towel, Melena's eyes fluttered open. Her gaze locked on his. Had she seen the lust in his expression before he blocked it out? He got his answer when she gasped, grabbed hold of his wrist, and whispered. "Make love to me."

Theo's body was more than ready. But, his mouth wouldn't cooperate. "No."

"No?" Her voice husky, her eyes dark with want, her skin flushed with need. She rose from the bed and moved to stand naked in front of him. Twisting slim fingers into the dark mat of hair that covered his chest, she stood on tiptoe to trail feather-light kisses along his neck. She sighed and tucked her head beneath his chin before wrapping her arms around his waist and pressing her body against his. *Sweet Jesus.*

"What do you mean 'no'? Didn't you say I was an itch you couldn't scratch? Well, I'm offering, Theo. I need this, too. Scratch me."

"Ah, give me strength." He uncurled her arms from around his body, placing her solidly away from him. "Go to bed, Mel. The answer is still no."

"Why, Theo?" Melena's skin paled, her eyes becoming bottomless pools of hurt. "I thought you wanted me. Wanted us."

"You thought wrong. I don't want you, not like this. When we sleep together, it won't be because you're running away from reality and looking for some mindless diversion."

"I don't think of you that way. Honestly, I don't."

"Look, I didn't think a harmless flirtation would get you so aroused. Get over it, sugar. The sexual anxiety plaguing your system is chemical, from the adrenaline high you're coming down from after being attacked. I'm not your therapist, and I'm not about to take advantage of this situation. You'll just have to satisfy those sexual urges on your own."

Melena flinched as if he'd struck her. The wounded look on her face was almost his undoing. He had to stay the hell away from her. Otherwise, he would lose all reason where she was concerned. When he wanted sex, there were a hundred names to choose from in his little black book. Her name would *not* be added to those pages.

"I'm your lawyer. This is business, nothing more. You're in trouble, and I'm trying to get you out of it in one piece." He forced his eyes to skim her body with cool indifference, as if the sight of her didn't drive him insane. "Try to keep your hands off me in future. I don't want to hit you with a sexual harassment suit."

He spun on his heel and left the room, slamming the door with a force that rattled the windowpanes. He stopped long enough to grab a bottle of Jack from beneath the bar. Then he stormed out into the night with Dood limping by his side. He intended to nurse his aching libido. Put thoughts of Melena out of his mind. It could never work between them.

He unclipped the cell phone from his waistband when he reached the swimming dock. Dialing his brother, he settled on an Adirondack chair then picked up the bottle.

MELENA DIDN'T CRY HERSELF to sleep that night. It wasn't that she didn't cry. She cried bucketfuls, until her eyes swelled and she could barely see. She just did not sleep. By five in the morning, she still tossed, turned and twisted in the sheets. Her cheeks flamed with embarrassment over Theo's rejection. She must have been out of her mind to throw herself at him based on a stupid dream. He had set her straight fast. He wanted nothing to do with her. She was business, nothing more.

To hell with him and the horse he rode in on. She didn't need Mr-Hotshot-Attorney-Knight-In-Shining-Armor-At-Your-Service.    She didn't need him one little bit.

Five minutes later, she was dressed in shorts and a tank top, out of the house, and leaving the boathouse by canoe. Doc had mentioned the inlet to the lake was a great place to see wildlife, if you went early enough in the day. Well, it wouldn't get any earlier than this for her.

She intended to spend the morning alone, retrieve some small scraps of pride, and salvage what was left of her fragile ego. With the sunrise a vibrant streak on the horizon, she paddled across the bay and into the mouth of the inlet.

The water was tranquil, a soft mist swirling its mirrored surface. She inhaled the beauty around her, a respite for her tortured soul. The glow of daybreak followed her deeper into the twists and turns of the creek, the occasional plunk of her paddle the only sound out of place. The warble of a loon called to her from a distance.

She almost tipped the canoe at the sight of a white-tailed buck emerging from a nearby stand of pines. Its antlers gleamed as he raised his head to watch her float by. Farther along, a heron swept low over the water to scoop a fish from the shoals, and otters played at the juncture of a feeding stream, rolling and diving. Their antics made her unwind, helped her forget life was so serious.

A snake eyed her from a rock face while shedding its skin. Melena suppressed a shudder. The snake wasn't poisonous, but the darn thing had to be at least five feet long. Deeper in the marshland, a mallard duck flapped its wings, squawked a warning to its brood, and herded the babies to safety among the reeds. She wasn't sure if the warning was because of her or the snake.

A beaver dam loomed in front of her, blocking the narrowing tributary. There was no way beyond it unless she portaged the canoe across the dome-thatched roof. Tying up to a lower branch of the dam, Melena caught a flash of red at a previous bend in the stream. Another canoe. Someone had followed her, paddled in silence through the marsh behind her. *Campo?*

She didn't waste any time. She scaled the beaver dam and plunged back in the stream on the opposite side. Keeping to the water to hide her tracks, she slipped across the rocky streambed, growing terror pushing her forward. Her only saving grace was the twisting curves of shoreline that hid her from Campo's view.

This was crazy. She was heading the wrong way. She had to double back. To go further was madness, the marsh grasses were thickening, leeches attaching themselves to her legs. *Ugh!* No time to think about that now. Campo was following. If he caught her he would beat, rape, and kill her.

Veering sharply away from the streambed, Melena crawled through the underbrush until she reached the shelter of trees. Barely breathing, she crouched low and waited for sounds of her pursuer. She slipped her cell phone from its waterproof fanny pack. No signal, she was in a dead zone.

Theo wouldn't ride to the rescue this time. She was on her own. After several minutes without hearing sounds of anyone following, she regained her feet and sprinted back through the marsh, this time heading in the right direction.

Reaching the beaver dam in record time, she paused to swat at the leeches glued to her legs, their bodies growing fatter by the minute. Wanting to scream, the unmistakable sounds of splashing feet refocused her attention. Campo wouldn't give up. Melena jumped into her canoe, pushed off, and paddled with all her strength.

Panicked, she veered left instead of right at the mouth of the inlet. She stroked against the current, instead of the opposite way toward the cottage and safety. Hysteria bubbled as she realized her mistake. There was nothing for it, she had to continue and pray for a miracle. There were no houses along this stretch of shoreline, no one to hear if she screamed for help. She hazarded a quick glance over her shoulder. The lake was rough, the red canoe gaining fast in the distance. Battling high winds, the waves tossed her further from shore.

"Melena! Stop!"

*God in heaven. Campo!* His voice followed, mocking her as she battled the waves to escape him.

Her collarbone ached from the stab wound of the previous night. The stitches pulled taut as she struck out for a small break in the rocks ahead.

She was physically fit, jogged on a regular basis. If she could make it to shore, she could outrun him, get to high ground where her cell phone would work, then hide in the forest until help arrived. Theo would look for her, once he discovered she was missing.

*Theo.*

God, she had it bad for him. Even when she was running for her life, he stayed in her thoughts. He would blame himself if anything happened to her because of last night, because of his cruel words to her. Because she had run off like a fool on her own.

Trees flashed by, the currents converged, pushing her back the way she had come. She fought to steer the bow toward shore. Gusts of wind blew her farther off course and closer to the evil pursuing her. Campo would cut off any means of escape.

Tipping the canoe, Melena swam with powerful strokes. Soon the rocky bottom greeted her, scraped her legs, and promised her that land was only a few strokes away. She heaved to her feet, broke into a run, tripped, and almost fell. Her shoe snagged something hidden in the weeds. Panicked, she grabbed at rocks to steady herself.

Her gaze shot to the object trapping her foot. *What the hell?*

Campo. Or what was left of him lay in the shallows; his pale skin waxy, his eyes clouding over, a small hole in his forehead.

Heaven help her, he was dead!

Melena covered her mouth, refusing to throw up. She couldn't stay here. She had to move before whoever was chasing her caught up.

Campo might not be able to hurt her anymore, but that didn't mean his partners wouldn't.

Reaching the relative protection of forest, she whipped out her cell phone and got a signal this time. Her hands shaking, she stared at the glowing screen. God, she didn't know Theo's number.

She dialed 9-1-1 instead. A woman answered. She identified herself and told the dispatcher about finding Campo's body. She was about to explain that she was being chased when a tree branch cracked close by. Her words jumbled with terror as fear overrode sanity.

For God's sake, she didn't even know where she was! The dispatcher told her to stay on the line so they could triangulate her cell's GPS signal. The sounds of leaves crunching underfoot magnified and Melena flat-out panicked. She cut and ran.

An old logging road stretched up ahead. She tore through the underbrush to reach it, ignoring the scratches on her arms, the tears in her clothes and leech marks stinging her legs. Pounding the uneven ground beneath her feet, she raced for survival.

Police cars roared up the road, slamming on their brakes. Bar lights flashed. Sirens blared. Four officers leapt from their cruisers and raced toward her. *Hallelujah!*

One of the uniforms loomed in front of her, gun drawn. "Put your hands behind your head. Get on your knees."

"W-what?" Melena spun on her heels, glancing over her shoulder. No one was behind her.

"Get down. Do it!"

Everything spiraled downhill from there. She was shoved to the dirt, handcuffed behind her back.

She screamed and tried to explain. "There's a man in the woods...there's a man chasing me!"

A cop had a knee braced against the small of her back which hurt. She fought like a mad woman, tried to shake him off. Suddenly, Sully appeared in her periphery. *Thank God!*

He flashed his badge and tossed the burly cop aside. "Get off her."

Hoisting her to her feet, he had the cuffs removed, grabbed her arm, and marched her straight to his Tahoe. "Get inside, don't move, and keep quiet."

He slammed the door and followed the others down to the lake.

# Chapter 14

The cell phone rang and Theo rolled out of bed. He didn't want to answer. His mouth tasted like a barroom floor from the cigars he'd smoked and Jack he'd poured down his throat last night. He had a king-size hangover and kicked himself for letting his guard down. He had been stupid.

As frustrated as he was, he never should have tied one on. Melena would have paid the price if anyone came looking for her while he was passed out in a drunken stupor. He reached for the phone when it started ringing for the third time, snarled his best imitation of a beast from hell. "What?"

"Your client needs you ASAP, bro. How in God's name did she shake loose on her own like this?"

"What are you talking about?" Theo's blurry vision cleared, allowing for a quick room-to-room search of the house. Sully was right. Melena had flown the coop.

His brother filled him in on what had gone down while he had been oblivious to everything but the drums pounding in his head and the river of liquor burning holes in his gut. "You'd better get over here and take control of your client fast. Before the locals toss her in the slammer and throw away the key."

"Damn woman." Theo hustled for the shower, his toothbrush, and a change of clothes. Even as he did so, the little voice in his head made a detour through the guilt sector of his brain and claimed full responsibility for Melena's actions. This wasn't her fault.

A HALF HOUR LATER, he moored the Bayliner behind an outcropping of rocks, out of sight. He hauled ass overboard and jogged across the small peninsula. Adjusting his sunglasses to filter the sun's glare, he followed the sounds of voices and frantic activity.

He locked his attention on the far shoreline where he knew the body had been found. Splashes on nearby foliage suggested more than one rookie had already heaved their stomach contents while viewing the scene. Thank God, he hadn't eaten today. He knew from experience that floaters could be bad. He had seen his fair share of them in countless tours of duty with Special Ops.

It wouldn't be cool to retch all over his shoes if the body was ripe, particularly when he was legal counsel to the person of interest caught red-handed fleeing the scene.

*Oh, yeah, this day just keeps getting better and better.*

With the sun clearing the mountain peaks, he exhaled on a groan and wondered if Melena would be in lock-up by breakfast time. The truth was he was glad the twisted deviant was dead. He would have killed Campo himself for what the man had done to her, if he'd only had the chance.

Moving down a wooded slope to reach the scene without disturbing potential evidence, he noticed the uniforms congregated on the shoreline. Murder overshadowed the beauty of landscape and blue skies as he advanced and came face-to-face with his brother.

Sully cocked his head and Theo followed him away from the local cops. "Where's my client?"

"Safely squirreled away for now. She was caught fleeing the scene and put up quite a struggle. The cops came down hard on her, bro. They say she called it in from her cell phone, even identifying Campo as the corpse. Then she tried to take off before the law arrived."

Theo ground his back teeth at the stupidity of her actions. "What in blazes was she thinking?"

His brother shrugged. "Maybe she wasn't thinking at all. She could have flat-out panicked. Being alone in the wilds with a corpse is enough to freak anyone out."

"Sure," Theo snorted, "if we were talking about any normal person. But *that* woman has Teflon balls. I don't see her turning tail and running from a dead man."

"You could be right," Sully acknowledged with a grin. "It was just dumb luck I got curious and followed the cruisers when they blew by me on the highway. The first responders had her tackled to the ground and handcuffed by the time I rolled up. Slightly overzealous, considering no charges have been laid."

Sully nodded in the direction of his SUV, angled halfway in a ditch alongside a rutted logging trail. "I flashed my badge, threw my weight around, and stashed her out of sight until you got here. I'm sorry as hell, Theo."

"Hey, it could be worse. Thanks for the quick heads up." Theo grimaced as he processed his surroundings, pumping his hands into fists. "This isn't the primary crime scene. There's no blood anywhere. It's a dump site, for pity's sake. What? They want to arrest her for tripping over Campo's corpse?"

"I agree, but I have to play nice with the locals since this isn't my jurisdiction. Montreal is miles off this beaten track, and I am supposed to be here on vacation. I can only push the envelope so far." Sully pressed the bridge of his nose between thumb and forefinger. "Wait until you meet the sergeant-in-charge over there."

Theo's eyes cut to the uniform standing some thirty feet away. The fool's arms waved through the air like a bird taking flight. He barked orders to his underlings, who trampled potential evidence in their efforts to do his bidding.

"The dickhead doesn't know his ass from his elbow," Sully muttered under his breath. "He hasn't even viewed the body yet. He's waiting on the Medical Examiner to take him by the hand, give him a rough estimate as to time and cause of death, before he decides if he is charging Melena with a crime or not."

"Unbelievable." Theo choked back a string of curses as he further surveyed the scene. "Any fool starting training academy could see the third eye planted in Campo's forehead. A .22 caliber slug, judging by the diameter of the entry wound. A second one to the heart. Double taps...execution style. Not to mention Campo's eyes have filmed over and the fish have been nibbling."

Theo rubbed his eyes before turning his gaze to his brother. "No crime scene and it's obvious this isn't a fresh kill; he probably died last night after he failed to nab Melena at *Charlie's*. And you are telling me the sergeant needs the ME's opinion to sort through the clues? Man, this does not bode well."

Sully shot him a dark look. "No kidding."

"Look, even if she did kill this pond scum—and that's a very big *if*—I can argue she was defending herself." Decision firing his blood, Theo pivoted to make tracks for the Tahoe.

"Unless she has the murder weapon stashed in her bra, which I highly doubt, I'm taking her out of here. The sergeant can't hold her without evidence. Tell that jackass to catch a boat ride down the lake when he's ready to question her. We'll be waiting."

By the time Theo reached the SUV, he was ready to slice and dice anyone in his path. It was partly out of fear for Melena, but also because of the bull-headed foolishness of her actions. He told himself it had nothing to do with the attraction between them. It also had nothing to do with his asinine behavior last night, the reason she had given him the slip and gotten into this mess in the first place.

He wrenched the door open. Melena glanced up, looking as bedraggled and beautiful as a woman could look with leaves stuck in her hair, scratches on her face, and mud saturating her clothes.

She tipped her chin in defiance, her icy cobalt-blues flashing a stay-away-if-you-know-what's-good-for-you warning. Satisfied she wasn't hurt, he ignored the warpath signals and dragged her to the ground beside him. When she protested, he clamped a hand over her mouth and hissed in her ear.

"Not one word, sugar. Keep your head down and get moving. We're out of here."

MELENA WANTED TO BREATHE fire but knew better than to argue. Theo was in a snit. The way he acted, she knew he thought this was all her fault. Finding Campo's body had not exactly thrilled her either.

She'd been terrified. Someone had chased her. The least he could do was show a little compassion. But no, that would require him to have feelings for her. He evidently didn't care about her at all. But, was it possible he believed she was guilty?

Theo pushed her ahead of him, up a wooded knoll and down the other side like she was roll-away luggage. She wanted to tear a strip off him for the strong-arm tactics. Instead, she clamped her lips shut and stumbled along as he shoved her over rocks and through waist-high water to reach the Bayliner.

The final insult came when he hoisted and pitched her into the stern like a beached whale. She landed on the carpet with a thud as he followed her over the side.

"Stay down," he ordered, slapping her backside as he moved forward to turn on the blower to clear the gas fumes in the bilge.

"Why? So, the cops won't see me?" she taunted. "They will eventually realize I'm not in Sully's Tahoe."

"I don't give a rat's ass about the cops." He turned off the blower, keyed the engine, tapped the throttle, swung the bow away from shore, and headed for open water. "I just don't want you getting the seats dirty."

He had the nerve to laugh after he tossed out the insult. Temper spiked her pulse like a jackhammer. Theo was a burr on her backside, an arrogant pain in the ass.

But, she wondered—oh, how she wondered—what would their relationship be like if circumstances were different. And how in the world had her life come to this?

THEO SPOONED IN ENOUGH coffee grounds to make mud, added water to the pot, and flipped on the gas jet. Melena stared into space while he worked, exhaustion overriding anger, shored up by the refrigerator pressing against her back.

Caring about him hurt. His cruel, well aimed insults last night had hit the bull's-eye. How dare he blame her for today's events when *he* was the one who had virtually pushed her out the door by being such a jackass? She refused to feel guilty.

He crossed the floor to her side and laid a hand on her shoulder, steering her toward the nearest chair. "I want to take a look at those marks on your legs."

Low on his haunches beside her, his fingers probed along an outer thigh. "How did you get these?"

Too tired to pull back, too needy to push him away, she allowed his examination. In spite of the adrenaline letdown after finding Campo's body this morning, Theo still managed to arouse her with an impersonal touch. He sent out signals filled with blatant lust. Yet, he had accused her of sexual harassment last night. What was his problem?

After all, wasn't he the one who had carried her from the tub? Hadn't he dried her naked body with a towel while she still slept?

Hadn't she awakened to the heat of his gaze on her skin, as if he'd wanted to bury himself deep inside her? Or had she imagined all of it?

She massaged her temples. The whole episode was a never-ending nightmare. "Just forget about it. I have worse things to deal with right now than bloodsucker bites and a couple of scratches."

"I can't ignore what happened." Cupping her face, Theo grazed a knuckle against her cheek. "I was out of line last night. Way out of line. The things I said to you were brutal and definitely not true. I wanted you so badly I choked up. Panicked big time, and shoved you out of reach because I couldn't trust myself. I'm not used to wanting a woman for anything other than sex. And with you, it's different."

*Get real*, she thought, even as her heart pumped hope into her chest. "I don't understand you. What I do know is horrible things keep happening to me. I have no control over any of them. These crossed signals you keep sending me are not helping, so figure out what you want, Theo. I can't keep doing this."

"I know, sugar." His mouth covered hers, the faint taste of liquor betraying his sins. Had he gotten drunk while she had held her own pity party last night? Both of them miserable?

"You make my head spin, Mel. I want you so badly I can't seem to focus on anything else." Big hands ran down her arms, lightly brushing the sides of her breasts. Then he bent to her leg, caressing her calf, licking a path along the suction marks made by the leeches, his eyes never leaving her face.

"I have feelings for you. Strong feelings. More than I can wrap my mind around. I can't afford to act on those feelings yet, not when my first priority is keeping you alive."

A low moan escaped her, before a buzzing sound snapped her back to reality. "Your cell phone is ringing."

Theo cursed, released his hold on her leg, unclipped the phone from his belt, and checked caller ID. "Talk to me."

Several minutes passed as he paced the kitchen, phone to his ear. Eyes cutting briefly to hers, crease lines furrowed his brow. He cupped his hand over the phone. "Why don't you grab a shower? Sully and I have a few things to do. I'll drop you with my parents while I'm gone."

"Not on your life, Sparky. I will *not* be babysat by your family." She shoved by him to turn off the coffee, jabbing a finger in his chest. "I'm going with you."

"Not this time."

Mel rinsed off in very cold water to cool down. Theo's hands on her in the kitchen, the feel of his mouth sliding up her leg had shaken her. Her life was a mess. And the sexual inferno heating up between them was insanity. She shook her head, quickly cleared those thoughts away, and shouted through the bathroom door. "Leaving me with your family will only endanger them. I'm going with you and Sully."

Call it instinct, but she knew something wasn't right.

She dressed in her usual garb, shorts and a T-shirt, ran a comb through her hair, and rushed onto the deck where Theo waited for her. His facial expression shut down when she marched up to him. "Just spit it out and get it off your chest. What's going on?"

"I asked Sully to run a check on Tom Sawyer last night, after the attack on you at the bar."

"And what did he find?"

Theo pulled her down beside him on a chaise, took her hands in his, and nailed her with a glance. "The first twenty years of Sawyer's life are blank. In other words, he created a whole new identity for himself when he was twenty-one years old."

"Sawyer is using someone else's identity?" Mel searched Theo's eyes for a glimmer of what was to come. "Why would he do that?"

"There's only one reason I can think of. Sully has connected the dots between Sawyer and a plane crash in the Rocky Mountains. It's the plane crash that killed your father. No trace of Ken Davidson was ever found."

"M-my father's remains were never found? And shortly afterward Tom Sawyer's persona came into being?" She felt the blood drain from her face and would have keeled over, if she hadn't already been sitting down. "You believe he's my father, don't you? That Tom Sawyer has risen from Ken Davidson's ashes?"

"It's a long shot, but it's starting to look that way."

"Holy, holy cow." Blood seemed to coagulate in her veins, her body near to frozen with shock. Tom Sawyer could be her father? Did that mean he had come here to hurt her for the inheritance? No, that didn't make sense. Not when he had protected her from those goons at *Charlie's* last night.

Theo said nothing. He held her in strong arms, stroked lazy circles along her spine, and allowed her the time to weave the mother lode of all shockers into the tapestry of her newly defined life.

Yep, the last few weeks had been a pip. Not only had she discovered she was adopted, but she'd had a grandmother, a woman who had been killed before she'd had the chance to know her.

Added to that, she was a suspect in her grandma's murder. Then there was her biological father, the black sheep of the family, also dead. Well, he was *supposed* to be dead. Now it seemed he may not be as dead as everyone thought.

Not to mention the attacks on her by Campo, the fact she could still be charged with his murder, and no one knew who had hired him to assault her in the first place.

*Sweet destiny's child.*

She buried her face in Theo's shirt, soaking in his strength and warm masculine scent. She really didn't know whether to laugh or cry, though neither would do her any good. No, only action could help her now. Minutes later, she released her chokehold on Theo and hauled herself to her feet. "I want to see what Sawyer has to say for himself. Let's go."

The boat ate up the waves with dizzying speed, Theo one-handing the steering wheel while taking his Glock from the glove box. Sully rode shotgun with Melena delegated to the back of the boat. If either man spoke, she couldn't hear what they said above the engine's roar. But she could read their thoughts. Stoic body language said it all. The big, brawny men would protect the little woman from the evils of the world.

*Not this time, guys.*

Clouds chased the afternoon sky while darkness permeated her brain with depressing thoughts. She prayed and prayed.

*Please, don't let Tom Sawyer be my father.*

"Are you sure you want to do this?" Theo's assessing gaze caught hers and held firm as he handed her from the Bayliner. "Just say the word and I'll take you back. It's not too late."

"I don't have a choice, Theo. I need to know the truth." Running a hand through her hair, Melena noticed how badly it shook. She tried to relax and mellow out a little bit. Nothing worked; it was too late for that. A root canal sounded like more fun than facing off against Tom Sawyer. Still, she had to hear his answers for herself.

"Stay close," Theo warned. He slammed through the door unannounced, keeping her safely off to the side while Sully scanned the woods around the small cabin. The interior swallowed her whole when she entered; the room was stifling and airless like a tomb.

Sawyer sat with his back to the far wall, facing her, his Sig Sauer in plain view on the tabletop. He made no attempt to go for the gun when they rushed the room.

"I've been expecting you." The man swept a hand in their direction. "Pull up a chair."

Sully moved behind them, bolted the door, and leaned against the doorjamb. Theo guided her to the table, settled her across from Sawyer, and palmed the Sig before seating himself.

His face a mask of cool indifference, Theo barely even blinked. If he was right, Tom Sawyer was not only her father but the reason her life was in danger. He eyeballed Sawyer with a thunderous look. "Do you have anything to say to Melena before I rip your heart out?"

"Yes, but first..." Sawyer bent low over a small mirror on the table and removed his contact lenses. When he raised his head, his eyes were a startling cobalt-blue, the same shade as her own. She had always wondered where the unusual hue of her irises came from. Mystery solved.

"For what it's worth, I'm sorry, Melena. I wish with all my heart things could be different for you. But, it is what it is. I am your father."

She stared at him while struggling to breathe. Thank God Theo didn't touch her, although she knew he wanted to. Compassion lined his face and willed her to have courage. Or was it pity she saw in his eyes, disappointment over the dysfunction of her family?

Her heart filled with an inexplicable rage at the thought. She wasn't responsible for the events leading up to this shit storm in her life. A hand shot out. Her fist connected with Ken Davidson's jaw with a resounding thwack. And a lot of pain to her knuckles.

*Take that, you bastard, for every lousy thing you have ever done!*

"Don't flatter yourself. *You* are not my father. My father is the loving man who gave me his name and raised me from birth. *You* are nothing but a sperm donor."

"Touché. I deserved that." Davidson rubbed a palm along his jaw and grunted. "You've got a bite to you, and that's good. Because you're going to need all the strength you have right now. What I'm about to tell you isn't pretty."

"Cut the rhetoric and get to the punch line," Theo snarled. "What the hell is going on, Davidson, or whatever your name is?"

"I'll get to that. Perhaps your brother would move to the table and be part of this conversation. We need all the help we can get to see Melena safely through this."

Sully edged farther into the room as Ken—Melena couldn't think of him as her father—got down to the facts.

His voice cracked as he spoke of his involvement with Angelo Vincelli and the money he had skimmed while working in Vincelli's organization. He had been a pilot for Vincelli, flying blood money from one location to the next. Until the night he had seized the opportunity to cut his losses and make a new life for himself. He had bailed out of his Cessna in a snow squall before it crash-landed, taking enough of the cartel's money to make him a rich man.

"Vincelli somehow figured out you're still alive, Ken. He's coming after your daughter to smoke you out," Theo said softly, menace clipping each syllable with deadly intent. "Maybe I should kill you myself and send him the body. Problem solved."

"Yeah, you should. It's what I deserve." Davidson eyed him with a dull glance. "But, there's more Melena needs to hear while I'm still breathing."

The sound of a plane flying low overhead pierced the quiet of the cabin. Ken Davidson—*her father*, she reminded herself—moved to the window to scan the horizon, then turned in her direction. "It's time you knew the truth, Melena. All of it."

He paced in front of her, his movements creating a draft, his hands punctuating the air for emphasis. "What Theo said is true. I'm the one who set the dogs on you...the Vincelli cartel."

Melena swallowed the nausea churning up the back of her throat, then held up a hand to keep Theo planted firmly in his chair. She wanted to sob over her father's confession, but held back the tears, gulping in air until she had herself under control. "There are a lot of other things you still haven't told me. What else?"

A pained expression twisted Ken's face. He scrubbed it away with the back of a hand. "I have so many regrets. But none more than the decision I made when I gave you up."

She ignored the comment, not wanting to believe him, and fought to keep her voice level. "Where is my mother?"

"Marla died in childbirth." Davidson's eyes visibly softened, tears spilling over the rims when he turned her way. "She had a spark that simply took my breath away. Like you do now. Seventeen years old, and just out of high school. I was eighteen. I took her to the prom that year and later...well, we fell in love."

"Sit down and tell me the rest of it," Melena said. "You owe me that much."

Ken sank to his chair, his legs splayed in front of him, his hands gripping the tabletop. "Before we knew it, your mother was pregnant. We hid the pregnancy for the first few months while making plans for the future. I'd been running backroom poker games for some local fellas and I knew my particular skills could land me a job in one of the casinos in Las Vegas, so we headed there."

Her father's chest heaved. "I got a job right away, except we didn't have enough money for medical care for Marla. She never saw a doctor until I took her to the hospital that day to give birth."

His face went white as a sheet, his voice fractured. "There...there were complications...and your mother died."

"My mother died, so you threw me out like a disposable diaper?" Anger threatened to boil over. Melena fought it back, hid her pain, determined to keep her feelings from him. "Gee thanks, *Dad*."

Her father looked miserable. "Look, I can't ask you to forgive me, Melena, but you need to understand that I did what I thought was right for you, and not just for me." His hand reached across the table and held firm. She waved Theo off when he would have broken her father's grip on her arm.

"Honey, I was a kid torn up with grief. I had just lost the love of my life. And suddenly, there you were—a defenseless infant—a tiny replica of Marla. A reminder of the woman I had lost. I didn't know how to take care of you, and I was too proud to go to my family, or Marla's. But, she still has family in Montreal if you're interested in meeting them."

Melena was hard-pressed to decipher which emotion for her father was the strongest at that moment: disappointment, betrayal, hatred, longing, love? Dissolving in a puddle of anguish would have to wait. She would be damned if she'd let him know how much she hurt because of him.

Her father continued, "I guess you pretty much know the rest. I went to a lawyer in Montreal, someone recommended to me who specialized in private adoptions. Your parents adopted you, and I walked away with enough seed money to start over. I headed back to Las Vegas and tried to forget, ended up working for the Vincelli cartel. Angelo Vincelli took me under his wing and got me my pilot's license."

He leveled a heartfelt gaze on her then. "The sad truth is I didn't have any allegiance to my family in those days. I was too busy looking out for number one. By the time I grew up and realized what I had done, it was too late to make it up to you and start over.

"Now, I have nothing left but agonizing regrets. Melena, it's my fault your grandmother is dead and you've been hurt so badly. And I swear I will give my life to keep you safe and away from Vincelli. Theo and Sully can fly with me to Las Vegas and hand me over to Angelo. I will return his money with interest and take my chances, providing the cartel agrees to leave you in peace."

"Nice thought, Davidson, but it won't work," Theo cut in. "How does the cartel know you're still alive?"

"That's anybody's guess, but I figure I was spotted in the Caymans when I made a recent deposit into my account. I noticed a man watching me who looked vaguely familiar from the old days. I don't remember his name, but he obviously knew me."

# Chapter 15

Theo fought the red haze of temper. He wanted to pound Davidson into the ground for all the grief he had caused both Sarah and his daughter. Still, the man might have some redeeming qualities, if he was willing to help Melena now. He also tied up a loose end; he had followed Melena in the canoe that morning to protect her from Campo, which meant he hadn't known the bastard was already dead.

"Vincelli can't be trusted to leave Melena alone, even if you do turn yourself in, so you can forget that idea." Theo slid the Sig back in Ken's direction. "You'll need this, because if you didn't kill Campo, the goon squad is here."

"I didn't kill him, although I would have if I'd had the chance. The cartel must have done it after he screwed up so many times with Melena."

"He missed me again with the others last night at the bar," Melena added, picking at an invisible thread on her shorts, and flashed Theo a wobbly grin.

God, she had to be scared out of her wits with her father suddenly thrust into her life, Campo and his goons attacking her, and now this business with Vincelli. Theo wished he could spare her all of it. He couldn't.

Sully nudged his elbow. "I don't think the cartel knows Davidson's at the lake, bro, or they would have already made a move on him."

Theo locked gazes with Melena across the table, his mind devising, and just as quickly discarding, possible scenarios. "They will know soon enough, if they haven't already spotted him. Meanwhile, let's keep him off their radar until we're ready."

"I know that look, bro. What's on your mind?"

"I'll let you know when I figure it out."

An hour later, Melena and Sully joined Theo around the table on Melena's deck, flipping through the adoption records that arrived by special messenger and boat taxi. The hospital birth records had also arrived, courtesy of a police buddy of Sully's in Las Vegas who had pulled the file and forwarded it on by email.

The joint paperwork told the tale. A female child had been born twenty-seven years ago to Marla Jones in Las Vegas. Ken Davidson was listed on the birth certificate as the father. Marla Jones had died in the hospital and, two weeks later, Ken had given the child up for adoption in Montreal.

"Davidson is telling the truth. He's your father."

Melena looked numb with shock. She pushed to her feet and moved for the stairs down to the dock. "I'm going for a swim."

Theo watched her go, her back ramrod straight, her fists clutched tightly by her sides. When she reached the lake, she shook off her cover-up and adjusted the ties of a red bikini. His gaze slid sideways until his guy parts were under control and he heard the splash when she dove in.

Lumbering along behind her, Dood eased himself down on the pier, following her powerful strokes through the water with a turn of his head, a swish of his tail, and a lot of whining. He didn't like her being so far out of reach. Neither did Theo.

The lake appeared calm for the moment, but a major storm was headed their way and would hit before nightfall, according to the latest weather bulletin.

Sully shook his head and took a swig of coffee. "Man, this has got to be tough on her."

"Yeah, that's putting it mildly." Adjusting his shades, Theo continued to watch Melena in the water. "Finding out she's adopted has to be mind-blowing, never mind the fact her father has mob connections that killed her grandmother and have put her own life on the line."

He ached for her. It was an impossible situation, one that would only get worse if something didn't happen soon. Keeping Melena safe was his bottom line.

"So, what's the game plan?"

"We need a meet with Angelo Vincelli."

Sully's eyebrows rose. "You never were one to let the grass grow under your feet. And just how will we draw this puke out into the open?"

"He'll show—after we catch the scumbags he sent here to do his dirty work." Theo's eyes cut to his brother and neither of them said a word for a full minute. "We hold the bargaining chip."

"That chip being Ken Davidson," Sully said, grinning.

"Right. Vincelli will want to finish off Davidson himself." After confirming Melena still swam nearby, Theo settled back in his chair.

"Vincelli is one powerful son of a bitch. We'll need help with this one, Sully. We can't use the local cops to bring him down, and I'm not about to risk Melena's life. Let's get some of our reserve military unit out here. I'm hoping Hawke can join the party, provided he has men watching Joelle."

"Don't worry about our little sis. Hawke has Joelle covered." Sully swore then banged a fist on the table. "Of course, I feel sorry for Hawke when she finds out, and she *will* find out. When she does, she'll flay and feed him to the sharks off of Galveston."

Theo laughed at the image, although he suspected his brother wasn't far off the mark. Joelle gave a whole new meaning to the word *obstinate*. He watched Melena pull herself to the dock and slide her cover-up over her head before he turned again to Sully.

"Our family, Ken Davidson, and Mel need protection twenty-four/ seven, and I don't trust anyone else to do the job except for our guys. Once our team's in place, I'm planning a little surprise for our visitors from the cartel."

"I'm on it." Sully reached for his cell phone and started searching the directory for numbers. "I knew there was a reason I'm still on vacation and technically off the radar with my homicide division. Sometimes the badge and red tape take too long to meet the need."

"Yeah, especially with Melena running out of time."

"Theo, what about the local cops? Do you want me to call in a few favors to keep them out of our hair?"

"I wouldn't. I don't think the local boys will run interference with us. The lake is big enough and they won't have boats or helicopters at their immediate disposal. By the time they get wind of any action, we should have everything contained with minimum risk of collateral damage. I don't want to think about what could happen if we involve local law enforcement."

"You're right there," Sully agreed. "The sergeant hasn't even shown his face to take Mel's statement after finding Campo's body. He's way out of his league on this one."

"WHAT'S GOING ON, THEO?" Detouring through the house to change clothes, Melena caught snippets of their conversation through the screen door and open windows. "You're making plans that involve me. I'd like to know about them."

Sully moved off to make some calls as Theo crossed the deck to her. He opened the door and drew her outside, dropping an arm around her shoulders and a kiss on her cheek.

"It's just a precautionary measure. We're getting some of our military unit together to give us a hand here. You need better protection than Sully and I can handle by ourselves. So does the rest of the family. We've got to settle this thing with the cartel, sugar."

Lord in heaven, she hadn't thought about the danger to Theo's family. If Vincelli's goons knew he was helping her, they would know Theo's family was his Achilles' heel.

"I should just get away from here. I couldn't stand it if anyone else got hurt because of me."

"Hey, look at me." Theo wrapped an arm around her waist and tipped her chin. He smelled like home to her, all sensuous heat and spicy male. "You are *not* responsible for any of this, Mel. This train has been roaring down the tracks for a while. Now we have to stop it, and this is the best place to take a stand. Sully and I know this lake blindfolded. It will give us the upper hand against anything Vincelli can throw at us."

"How? How are we going to stop it?"

"When I've figured that out, you'll be the first to know."

He winked, bent to kiss the top of her head, and released his hold on her. Melena felt as if all the warmth in her system drained out of her when he dropped his arms. He steered her gently in the direction of the doorway. "Scoot. Sully and I have to make a few arrangements. I'll be along in a minute and we'll have some lunch."

"Well, that's just great. The big, studly man has work to do and the little woman has been delegated to the kitchen to provide nourishment for his belly."

"Hey, if you're still offering, I can always delegate you to the bedroom where you can provide nourishment of another sort." A sexy grin slid across Theo's mouth. "Think of it as your duty to God and country. A man should never go into battle without the love of a good woman to give him the edge."

"Your pick-up lines need a lot of work, Sparky. That is the biggest crock of cow pies I have ever heard."

"God knows, I try."

Melena closed the screen door and called over her shoulder. "If that's the best you can do, I'll be inside preparing a feast for my hero...army rations for lunch."

"What? Don't do me any favors," he wisecracked.

The sound of his laughter made her smile. She shook her head. Yep, she was a goner for sure. Theo had slid inside her heart and wasn't letting go.

Needing a distraction, she got lunch underway and headed to the hutch for placemats and napkins. As she rooted around in the bottom drawer, her cell phone beeped with an incoming text. Finally, her parents were getting back to her.

Her fingers punched the keys to read it. The message wasn't what she expected. Her heart lurched with a sickening thud.

*The boat landing. Midnight tonight. Tell no one. Come alone or Sauvage dies. Then we'll go after his family. We have eyes on all of you.*

She reread the horrifying text, her skull pounding with every word, tears clouding her vision. *Oh, God, no. Not Theo.* Melena cupped her hand over her mouth. She loved him too much to lose him, to risk him in a battle started by her father.

And his family...dear God, the danger to them.

*Come alone.* Melena knew she had to. If she told Theo he'd play the hero, charge to the landing tonight, and risk losing his family in order to protect her. They would all die.

Desperation had thrown her into Theo's arms—*her* desperation. She had leaned on him for protection because there had been no one else. He had gained her trust, kept her safe. And she'd fallen for this good, decent man. A man she would gladly die for if it meant keeping him and those he loved alive.

Her gut clenched and almost sent her to her knees. She knew, without a shadow of a doubt, she would do whatever the cartel wanted. There was no other way.

Frantic thoughts flitted across her brain. She was in deep trouble here. Theo hardly let her out of his sight. How would she get to the boat landing tonight without him knowing?

Who could she ask to help her? The answer was no one. She couldn't trust his brother or the other members of his unit when they arrived. They would never allow her to surrender to the cartel. She was on her own.

She was still rooted to the floor when Theo's hands touched her shoulders. Already spooked, a scream lodged at the back of her throat and held fast. Theo nipped the side of her neck, giving special attention to that tender spot beneath her ear. She didn't move, just closed her eyes to hold back more tears. His breath fanned her cheek.

"Mmm, you smell good enough to eat." His arms surrounded her with a sense of loss, of what they might have shared if the situation was different. His hands moved to her hips, powerful hands that jarred her from the blackness of her thoughts.

Her warrior.

Her love.

When she didn't respond to his caresses, Theo noticed the cell phone in her hand. "Did someone call you?"

She turned in his embrace, shoved the phone in the pocket of her cut-offs. Smoothing a brief kiss on his chin, she choked on the hysteria that crawled up her throat. Surrounded by the iron feel of him, the compelling smell of him, it horrified her that those monsters would snuff out his light—all the life in him—like he meant nothing.

He'd protected her so often, stood strong when she hadn't been able to stand on her own. Now, it was her turn to be strong for him.

"It's n-nothing. I was just trying to contact my parents again. N-no answer."

"Is something the matter?" Theo scanned the room for signs of trouble, lightly pushing the hair away from her face and locking his gaze with hers. A hand slipped downward to rest against her throat. "You're trembling, sugar, right down to your pink-polished toes."

Melena tipped her chin and gave him a gentle kiss. She lingered a moment, let herself taste him before pushing away from his chest. "It's j-just the after-effects of finding Campo's body and then having to deal with a stranger who c-calls himself my father."

Theo nodded his understanding. "And this mess with the cartel must be a little tough to swallow."

Melena wanted to throw up. He had no idea of the terror backing the air up in her lungs. He could never find out. She felt his stare on her retreating back as she headed for the kitchen, praying he'd been fooled by her explanation for her nervous behavior. Still, she felt as pale as death and knew she had barely run two coherent words together without stuttering.

Quaking like a leaf in a twister, she rushed to serve their meal, although she knew she wouldn't be able to eat a bite. She was afraid for herself, but terrified for Theo.

A few hours later, the *whomp, whomp* of rotor blades from the approaching helicopter was barely audible over the roar of winds and torrential downpour obliterating the night sky. According to the latest weather report, this was the tail-end of a hurricane moving inland off the coast of Maine into southern Quebec.

Flashes of light streaked the sky around her, the scent of ozone making Melena's nose twitch. Hiding under the bed seemed like the smartest thing to do. Instead, she huddled beneath the overhang on her deck, watching Theo and Sully as they headed into the squall to join the men stepping off the pontoons of the helicopter that had landed at her dock a few minutes ago.

Lightning tore the sky again. Treetops tossed and branches flew, carried on the wind as easily as leaves on a soft summer breeze. Whitecaps drenched the rocks below with a snapping spray, crashing against the dock where the men fought for balance. Using guide ropes, they somehow managed to pull the whirlybird into the double-wide boathouse; lowering its doors from the brunt of the storm, keeping the helicopter away from prying eyes.

The men turned in her direction and sprinted the path up to the house. She supposed it was lucky the fog hadn't settled in yet, that Theo's friends were able to land safely in spite of the weather. But, lucky for whom? Certainly not for her, not if she wanted to deliver herself to the cartel and keep Theo alive.

She jumped when thunder shook the foundations of the cottage and almost bolted when the men gained the deck. Theo grabbed her arm and herded her inside in front of the others. "Sugar, you're going to catch your death standing out there."

*Catch her death*...his words echoed and rang true. She almost laughed, but gritted her teeth instead, forcing herself to remain calm. *Breathe in, breathe out. Smile at everyone. Otherwise, Theo will be on to you.*

She focused on the new arrivals, surprised the team all looked relatively normal when they clomped into the house, with a few notable differences.

They were all built like powerhouses, just like Sully and Theo. There wasn't a flak jacket in sight, but she assumed their body armor was neatly concealed beneath those dark Gore-Tex jackets and golf shirts.

No camouflage clothing, M-16s, ground-to-air missiles or hand grenades could be seen in the bunch, unless those were what they transported in the innocuous-looking go bags being secreted away in the back bedrooms of the house.

Shoulder and ankle holsters, handguns and knives weren't so easy to conceal. Melena swallowed hard. These men were a bonafide death squad with the man of her dreams leading the way. She prayed they'd be able to save themselves and Theo's family if things didn't go according to her plan.

Introductions were made over coffee and sweet rolls in the kitchen. Melena behaved like a domestic goddess; refilling cups and passing out pastries. Doodlebug sat by without a care in the world. It seemed to her the wolf had joined forces with the men as soon as doggie treats were offered.

Theo explained that each man had his own specialty, although all could pinch hit for one another if it became necessary. Melena swallowed the lump in her throat and scanned their faces. How would she escape unnoticed from so many watchful eyes?

Jake Hawkins was the pilot, a formidable, brooding man with good looks and smoldering hazel eyes, eyes that gave nothing away while seeming to peel away layers to reach her very soul. Melena realized this was the man who had an eye for Theo's and Sully's sister. She had heard the brothers talking about him.

The mechanic, Micah Rivera, was a wizard with electronics and an all around MacGyver type, credited with the same resourcefulness as the television secret agent.

Reece 'Rocket' Morgan was a demolitions expert, a quiet, soft-spoken giant who was also a civil engineer. Theo said he had joined the military and never looked back, but he suspected the man had never gotten over the woman he had left behind.

Lawrence Logan was their logistics genius. Anything the team needed in any part of the world, Law would get the goods and then some.

Their linguistics expert was a black-eyed ghost, named Hunter Ryan, who had infiltrated foreign countries without leaving a trace. He spoke six different languages and several dialects of those fluently.

As team leader, Sully assumed command of operations. He was responsible for the success of their missions and getting the men in and out of hostile territory in one piece.

Theo, however, was in charge of this mission, Sully handing over the reins to him. He was also the team's number one sniper, a man who could shoot the eye out of an eagle at a distance of several football fields strung end to end.

As the men set up their *war room* in the dining area an hour later, Mel brought in heaping plates of sandwiches, ice water and beer. She purposely made a nuisance of herself, wanting to know what the plans were, demanding too much detail, asking personal questions of the new arrivals—questions which they weren't prepared to answer.

"Sugar, how about letting us have a few minutes to get our heads on straight? Then we'll fill you in on the details." Theo's hand was firm on her back as he ushered her out of the room and closed the door.

Exactly the response Melena had hoped for. She raced to her closet, dragging on jeans, a thick sweater, and outer rain gear. Thrusting her feet into hiking boots, she stuffed her cell phone and a flashlight into the zippered pockets of her raincoat, all the while praying for a miracle.

High winds scraping branches against the house masked the sound of her escape through a bedroom window. Thunder boomed and the winds pitched to a screaming howl when she reached the dock.

Her little boat was ahead, rocking in the waves at its moorings, the automatic baler almost futile in its attempts to pump out the downpour filling the hull.

Melena unhitched the ropes from the circular rings and crawled into the vessel. But not before Dood gained the bow. The big lug planted himself on the bow seat, curling into a tight ball as protection from the pelting rain.

"Out of the boat, Dood!" The command earned her a *get serious* look from wise, gleaming-yellow eyes. The wolf groaned, closed his eyes, and buried his face in his tail, ignoring her instructions.

"Ooh, for heaven's sake. I don't have time to argue with you."

The choppy whine of the engine muffled by the storm, Melena engaged the gears and rounded the jetty. Once in open water, the waves pitched and rolled, broad-siding the boat until she swung about and attacked the whitecaps head-on. The baler whined, pumping out water slower than it poured back in.

Her feet were already soaked, her hands frozen to the throttle, an icy reminder she was still alive, at least until she got to the boat landing. With Dood along for the ride, maybe it would even out the odds a little.

A half hour later, she swiped the rain from her eyes and stared into the night. Nothing looked as she remembered it by daylight. Mountain peaks should have loomed on the horizon, guiding her along the waterway and keeping her safe from shore. Instead, she was surrounded by fog. The tall copse of pines standing guard at the mouth of the Narrows—the trees she so desperately needed to find in order to enter the channel—had disappeared.

The Narrows were treacherous, concealing hidden obstacles, unpredictable currents, and jagged shores. Theo had drilled the lesson into her often enough, had stressed that most rock formations were below the surface here, waiting to split the hull of any unsuspecting boat. The channel was also her only path to the boat landing. It connected this bay to the rest of the lake.

Melena glanced at her watch. She only had an hour to find Vincelli's men. She had never considered herself to be particularly brave, but she vowed she would protect Theo with her dying breath if necessary.

Picking up what little courage she had left, Melena fought the suffocating squeeze of her chest and eased the throttle forward.

If she didn't navigate the channel exactly as Theo had taught her, she would end up smashed on the rocks. She had to go on, needed a miracle to get to the landing before Theo realized she was missing. Maybe God would be merciful if she prayed hard enough.

Lightning flashed in front of her, shedding light on the mouth of the Narrows. Melena took it as a sign. No more thoughts of Theo and her love for him. There was no going back.

# Chapter 16

"The lady's nowhere to be found," Hunt announced after searching the house thoroughly. The others were back from scanning the perimeter of the cottage, the outbuildings, and the docks.

Hawke added grimly, "The small fishing boat is missing."

"Damn, she made a break for it," Theo said. "I told you, Sully, she's been acting weird since lunch."

"Yeah, you told me. What's the quickest way to find her?"

"We follow the wolf." Theo booted up his laptop. "Dood was guarding Mel while we were holed up in the dining room. He wouldn't leave her, and there's a tracking device imbedded in his collar."

"Theo?" Micah drawled as they waited for the computer to boot, "what's the story with you and this gal? I mean, I couldn't help but notice she is one gorgeous piece of—"

"Drag your brain out of your pants, Mic." Theo snapped. "Mel is mine. Understand?"

"I never thought I'd see the day." Sully moved behind his brother's chair and punched his shoulder. "It's about time, bro. And the family certainly approves of your choice."

"Yeah, well, the rest of you lug-heads have been forewarned. Keep your distance and your hands off of her."

"Don't worry," Micah winked and answered for the team. "We'll keep her safe and at arm's length at all times. But you can't blame a hot-blooded male, with eyes in his head, for trying. You are one lucky man, my friend."

*Lucky? Sure, if she doesn't get herself killed out there.*

A myriad of feelings overwhelmed him, the undeniable love he felt for Melena and his intense fear for her safety. He shoved those thoughts deep to concentrate on the job of getting her back. Without her in his life, he had a hunch he would be forever lost to recriminations of what they could have had. What he'd let slip through his fingers.

Once the laptop booted, Theo's fingers flew across the keys and lost no time getting into the tracking program. "There's Dood's signal. *Shit.* Mel's in the Narrows."

Hawke sensed the urgency. "Do we take the bird?"

"Can't. The wind shear is too risky and there's no place to land. But I want you to stay with the chopper. I'll call if I need her. The rest of us will go by boat."

Hawke nodded and started to move. "I'll get the Osprey ready in case we need her, too."

The Osprey was a rigid inflatable boat with a 65 HP outboard engine. It had come in handy many times with its ability to deflate and be transported on the helicopter.

"Good idea. Just keep her hidden in the boathouse. I don't want to raise any red flags for our mobster buddies. We need the element of surprise when they come for Mel."

Theo turned to Reece. "Grab your gear. We'll drop you at my place on the way. Although I doubt Vincelli's goons are stupid enough to be out in this storm, I'm worried about the rest of the family. Sully, you'll join Reece as soon as we find Melena. Take the Bayliner."

"Got it," Sully said, stuffing a first aid kit into his pack. "You can bring Mel back here in the two-seater while I continue on to Davidson's to drop off Mic and Hunt. Then I'll head for your place."

"That leaves me to follow Theo back here in Mel's boat?" Law asked.

"Right." *If it hasn't already been smashed to smithereens on the rocks.* Theo tamped down that idea with a growl. "Let's move."

"DOOD, I CAN'T SEE WHERE I'm going with you up on the seat like that. Get down. Now!"

Melena was chilled to the bone, her fingers flash-frozen to the throttle. Rain trickled inside the collar of her jacket. She shuddered, wanting to throw up her hands in despair and bawl her eyes out. At this rate, she would die of exposure before she was able to surrender to Vincelli's men. Theo would be killed if that happened.

There was almost zero visibility in the fog, worse since the lightning had moved off toward the mountains. Winds had battered the boat and thrown her off-course.

She felt every shuddering crunch, every grind of the propeller as it scraped and bounced its way along the rock-strewn bottom. One final chew and the prop stopped spinning. The motor shuddered and died. A backward glance over the transom told the ugly tale. The foot of the motor had completely sheared off.

Doodlebug climbed off the bow seat to settle against her, a paw brushing her knee. Even the wolf knew things weren't going well. "It's okay, boy. We'll be fine."

Melena's gaze cut forward, searching for some glimmer of hope. A menacing shape separated from the fog. The outline was huge, solid and wide, and positioned directly in the path of the crippled little boat. She lunged for a paddle, back-paddling to swing the bow and prevent a direct hit. The rock loomed larger, holding her gaze until something else caught her periphery.

A log submerged in the undertow clipped toward her with incredible speed. It rammed the boat portside and broke it apart, rivets in the hull popping like popcorn in a microwave.

In an instant, Dood knocked Melena over the stern, clamping down on her arm as he hit the water. Although her heavy clothes protected her from the full pressure of Dood's jaw, Melena started to sink from the weight. Dood held fast, lunged upward and regained the surface. He swam for the marker buoy at the center of the channel, ignoring her protests, dragging her along like a rag doll.

The buoy rocked and swayed, clanked on its anchor chains. With the last strength in her shuddering limbs, Melena grabbed onto the metal giant and hauled herself up. She twisted, grabbing Dood's collar to pull him up beside her. The buckle broke, the webbing slipped from her fingers. Melena screamed as the wolf disappeared beneath the waves.

THEO RACED AHEAD OF the Bayliner, running full-out in the sleek two-seater he had built a few years back. Lightning strikes had lessened now and moved inland, cutting his visibility. The winds still roared like a freight train. Rain hammered the windscreen faster than the wiper blades could do their job. The storm wasn't ready to play itself out.

He hauled himself out of his seat and took up position on the backrest, trying for an unobstructed view over the windshield. Slanting rain pelted his face, the peak of his ball cap doing little to protect his eyes.

*Where the hell is she?*

Usually, he loved challenging the elements and would have gone out in a storm like this for a lark. Not tonight. Not with Melena out there somewhere. The woman was pigheaded. Fearless. She didn't know when to quit. She was going to get hurt.

He didn't worry about the others behind him keeping pace. Sully knew the lake almost as well as he did. *Shit*, his brother could probably navigate the Narrows with his eyes closed. It was getting to Melena that mattered. The only damn thing that mattered.

Theo's hands gripped the controls as he flew across the water, the pulse in his jaw keeping time with each smack of the bow cresting a wave and jolting down hard on the other side.

What was Melena thinking to make this mad dash under the worst possible conditions? She was a novice to the lake. If she wasn't struck by lightning, she would almost certainly lose her way on the water, with miles and miles of desolate shoreline to keep her company. Or worse. Vincelli's men could be out there.

*Don't go down that road now. Focus on getting her back.*

He jerked back on the throttle and sank into the backwash, his boat settling at the mouth of the Narrows. Snatching up the laptop, he checked again for the GPS signal broadcasting from the wolf's collar. The signal was weak but flashing. A string of curses flooded the air around him. Dood was in the same location where he'd been twenty minutes ago. That meant Melena was still caught in the channel.

Abruptly, he noticed something else on the screen, something far more terrifying. In the blink of an eye, his worst fears hit home as his blood coalesced with dread. *Sweet Jesus God.*

Theo jammed the laptop under the seat and punched on the searchlight. Then he eased the throttle forward and rounded the first bend in the channel. As much as he wanted to gun the engine and get to Melena fast, he couldn't risk hitting her if she was out there floating around.

He prayed she *was* still out there floating around. Had she worn a life jacket? He knew she was a strong swimmer, but that wouldn't help her now, not if she had lost consciousness or snapped a limb fighting the rocks and water current.

He keyed his headset, willing some spit to loosen his tongue so he could get the words out without losing all control. "Sully, I'm in the channel now. Mel's got to be here somewhere."

"Say what?" Theo's shoulders tensed at the sound of his brother's disembodied voice. "How do you know she hasn't made it through the Narrows and gone out the other side?"

"Because Dood would never leave her, and his signal hasn't moved. The signal is underwater, Sully. Go slow...go real slow."

"Roger that. We'll find her, bro."

"I know we will." Theo heaved a sigh, his voice unsteady to his own ears. "Just pray she's alive."

He knew Sully and the other men understood the urgency of his transmission. Mel was either hurt...or they were looking for her dead body. A flash of light reflected off his rearview mirror. The Bayliner had moved into position behind him.

Fifteen minutes later, Theo neared the buoy at the opposite end of the Narrows without spotting Melena. Despite the floodlight, only fog reflected back at him, making it impossible to see beyond a few feet in any given direction. Her boat wreckage sloshed about on the waves and notched up the flames in his gut. Seeing a broken paddle, her life vest, and a cushioned boat seat had almost sent him careening over the edge. Melena should have been safely tucked away in her cottage. What had sent her out into this night?

He shouted her name for the hundredth time; his voice, and Sully's in the distance, raised above the howl of wind and drone of boat motors. Damn it, chances were they would never hear her small cries for help. They could pass by her in the swells without even seeing her. He felt powerless, but couldn't allow it to cloud his judgment.

The light from the marker buoy caught his eye. *Wait. What's that?*

Was he mistaken? Was that a flash of movement swirling in the mist? Or was it eye strain catching up with him? Theo edged closer to take a better look. His heart lurched when he recognized the fluorescent orange rain jacket, and Melena clinging to the buoy. He radioed the Bayliner to give them her location. Then he dropped anchor, stripped to his shorts and shallow dove over the side.

Melena took one look at him and plunged off the buoy in the opposite direction, floundering in her panic to get away. He could see her clothes dragging her down.

*What in blazes is the matter with her?* He closed the distance between them before she went under, grabbing her around the waist.

"Let go of me. Let me go!" Melena screamed and kicked out, still trying to swim away from him.

Theo held tight. He twisted her around and pinned her from behind, dragging her through the whitecaps to his boat. Hoisting her over the side, he climbed in behind her, shoving her into the seat when she tried to bail on him again.

"Are you out of your mind? What the hell is wrong with you?" Grabbing his jacket, he threw it around her and zipped it up, effectively pinning her arms to her sides. He clamped his thighs around her flailing legs. "Take it easy. Settle down."

"You don't understand! I need to...let me go," she yelled at him, a hysterical edge to her voice.

Stark terror widened her eyes, her breath coming out in choked sobs. She was as pale as a cadaver. It dawned on him it had a lot more to do with her proximity to him than the boat crash she had survived. Was she afraid of him?

"Oh, God! Please let me go. They'll...I can't...please, I have to go...oh, Jesus," she said between sobs.

Sully's voice cut in. Theo clamped a hand over her mouth so he could hear the transmission.

"Bro, is everything all right? We were rescuing the wolf when we heard Melena screaming. What's going on?"

"Ouch! Shit!" Theo shook free of her teeth, coming away with his chewed up fingers. "Sully, we're cool here, but I need to get Mel home ASAP. She's lost it...she's looking at me as if she'd rather be riding with the Son of Sam."

Sully laughed through the headset. "It must be that boyish charm you've got going for yourself. Can you handle her or do you need backup?"

"I'll take care of it. She only weighs a hundred pounds, and if all else fails, I'll just toss her back overboard."

*Gallows humor*, he silently acknowledged. Cops reverted to it, and so did special ops guys, when they rode high on adrenaline and needed to let off some steam. Surely to God Melena knew he wasn't serious.

Sully chuckled again. "I'll drop the other guys at Davidson's and then have Breeana take a look at the wolf. His stitches pulled loose. Do you want Doc to head over and take a look at Mel?"

"I'll call if I need him. Just drop Law off when you have time. The storm should keep Vincelli's boys away for at least a few more hours if they're around."

"Roger that. And bro...go easy on her. She's having a tough time."

Mel gasped when he thrust his hand against her chest and pinned her where she lay on the seat. Then he turned the key in the ignition, hauled anchor with one hand, and threw the boat in gear. Wind iced his body as they shot forward. He tried not to think about pneumonia setting in, but Murphy's Law, it was that kind of night.

"Turn around, Theo. I can't go back to the cottage. I need to go the other way!"

Theo spared Melena a glance as she lay beneath him, pale faced and spoiling for a fight. It was incredible how much she could try his patience in the space of five long minutes. He was freezing cold and madder than hell. And he just might take it out on her backside.

# Chapter 17

"What in heaven's name is the matter with her?" Hawke tied off the boat and stared up at Theo as Melena glared at both of them from the passenger seat. He stuffed an evil looking gun back in the holster under his jacket. "I could hear her screaming all the way from the house. What the hell did you do to her?"

"What did *I* do to *her*?" Theo ripped the keys from the ignition, leapt to the dock, and shook his head. "I have no idea, man."

He fisted his hands on his hips and glowered, exhaling loudly before looking down again at her. "Can you crawl out of there on your own or do you need help?"

She buried her face in her hands. "I'm not going anywhere. Give me the boat keys. Please!"

Theo stared at her, unable to mask his shock. He spoke softly. "Honey, if there is one thing I'm sure about, it's that I'm not handing over these keys."

Leaning into the boat, he held out a hand to her. She knew despair showed in her eyes. She couldn't move, just sat staring at him as though her life was over. Maybe it was.

He balanced on his haunches and scraped a hand over his jaw, his breath coming out in frustrated puffs. She seemed to be having that effect on him today. *Tough.*

"Mel, come on out of there so we can talk about this calmly. I don't know what's going on, but you're teeth are chattering and your lips are blue. You're going to be sick if you don't get into some dry clothes."

"N-no. You h-have to listen to me." She plastered herself against the far side of the hull, wiping her nose on a sleeve. She thought about jumping overboard, but what would that accomplish? She was numb with cold and probably couldn't swim a stroke to save her life. "If you don't give me those boat keys, your family is going to die!"

"You're not making any sense, sugar." Theo stayed where he was, crouched in front of her, eye-to-eye. "The only way you'll get your hands on a boat is if you come up to the house so we can talk about this calmly."

"We don't have time for that," she blurted, wishing her teeth would stop clacking together. "Vincelli's men are *here*. They're watching all of us now, even your family. If I don't go to the landing tonight and turn myself over to them, they will kill you and Sully, then your parents, Breeana and Cody. Please, Theo, you have to let me go!"

Hawke nodded at Theo and moved off toward the house. "I'll fill the guys in."

Theo bounced to his feet and loomed into the boat, hands on his hips. "Interesting scenario, but let's try another one on for size. It's easier for me to protect what's mine than to stand back and let the cartel have you. Why do you think the team is here?"

Mel blinked up at him. When Theo put it that way, it almost made sense. "But, Vincelli's text message said they had eyes on everyone—that they would kill you if I didn't meet them tonight."

Theo just smiled. "Well, maybe it did. But my family—even Ken Davidson—already have protection. Everyone is accounted for, Mel. They're all fine and they're going to stay that way. I doubt Vincelli factored in my guys when he sent you that message, since they arrived during the storm."

Theo reached down for her hands that were now free from his jacket and tugged her to her feet, lifting her bodily out of the boat before she could pull back.

An arm around her waist to support her, he steered her toward the house. He was right, she needed to get indoors and dry off. Her whole body was shaking.

"Correct me if I'm wrong," Theo said, "but didn't we agree early on that I'd handle the cartel and your safety? Why didn't you tell me about the text message?"

She rubbed at her temples and felt remorse tearing up her insides. "I d-didn't want to tell you. Knowing you, you'd charge out of here and get yourself blown to bits."

"Thanks for the vote of confidence." Theo opened the kitchen door and scooted her inside in front of him. He unzipped her out of his jacket before pulling off her rain slicker and hiking boots. Instant warmth.

"You can manage the rest yourself. Go grab a hot shower while I put on some soup. Then we'll talk some more."

She laid a hand on his arm. "I'm sorry. I totally messed things up tonight."

Holding her gaze a long moment, Theo shook his head then wrapped his arms around her. His mouth against the top of her head, he whispered, "*Shit*, woman. You scared the bejesus out of me."

"WHAT WERE YOU THINKING to take off like that, Mel?" Theo tossed back the beer he'd been nursing, stared out the living room window, and watched her approach in the reflection of the glass. The rain was finally easing off, the wind dying. Too bad he couldn't say the same about his heart hammering a hole in the wall of his chest.

Melena's breath hitched. She shot a tentative hand out to touch him as he guided her to the couch. "I really believed Vincelli would kill you. I couldn't stand it, Theo."

If he was reading her right, Melena had a *very* large stake in keeping him healthy. He should feel good about that, but he didn't. Not when he'd almost lost her.

"You took ten bloody years off my life tonight. Don't do it again."

"Theo, I..."

Melena looked like the picture of innocence in a dark blue sweat suit that almost matched her eyes. In spite of his anger, he was glad to see her color had returned. She had lost the ghostly pallor to her cheeks.

"Mel, I need to keep it together for all of us when we go up against Vincelli and his goons. I have to know you'll do as I say from now on."

"I'll obey your orders as long as I can carry my own weight," she argued. Her shoulders stiffened and she actually scowled. "I'm not some wilting violet you need to coddle."

"That's enough." He wheeled on her before she got another word out. "It's time you realized my team *kills* people like Vincelli. We're trained for it. We're the good guys, sugar, and we don't need you gumming up the works."

"When I tell you to hide under a bed or bury yourself in a pile of leaves, that's what you'll do. And that's *all* you'll do. You sure as hell won't be anywhere near the bad guys on this op, even if it means hog-tying and gagging you myself."

"You love this kind of action, don't you?" Her icy blue eyes blazed into his and she held her ground. "Just you and the guys against the vermin of the world. Well, get this straight, Sparky. Those bastards threatened everything, and everyone, that's important to me. I won't stand by while you take all the heat!"

No, he didn't enjoy the action. In fact, he hated it. But it was what he was trained for and what he did when there were no other options. He didn't want Melena tainted by that brush.

It was time to cut this conversation short and get her out of his hair. Piss her off so she wouldn't challenge him again.

"Are your shots up to date? Rabies, distemper, that sort of thing? Or should I rush to Doc to be treated for the chunk of my hand you tore off with your teeth?"

"Please. I'm trying to—"

"I'm through talking to you." He could see tears gathering on her lashes, a stricken look on her face. Hell, even her lower lip trembled. "Haul that little butt of yours off the couch and make tracks for the nearest exit. Stay put and out of my way and we'll get along fine."

Melena jolted. She looked like she wanted to say something more but lost her nerve.

"Go. Now."

She stumbled for the privacy of her bedroom and slammed the door. He watched her go, crushed his empty beer can, and chucked it into the wastebasket at the far end of the room.

*Way to go, asshole. Now you've scared her.*

Good. Maybe she'd forget this ridiculous idea of mixing it up with the cartel.

Theo headed for a refill in the kitchen, deciding that salsa and chips to go with his next beer were infinitely more interesting than anything Melena could have added to their argument.

"Well, what did she say?"

Theo popped the tab on his Molson and tossed a second one to Hawke. "What are you talking about?"

"Okay, buddy. Have it your way." Hawkins pushed away from the kitchen counter and folded his arms across his expansive chest.

"Stay out of this, Hawke. The woman is a nutcase to try and hand herself over to Vincelli. She's loony tunes, plain and simple."

Hawke said nothing, but instead gave Theo *the look*, what the guys liked to call his evil eye. If Theo wasn't careful, he knew Hawke would strip his psyche down to its bare elements. It was very unnerving for the individual under his microscope, laid open to Hawke like a corpse at an autopsy.

"What? Don't look at me that way. Once that woman's out of danger, I am so out of here."

"Why? Because she loves you? Because she tried to protect you? Or is it because you're nuts about her?" Hawke shook his head and opened the door to the back deck. "While I'm checking out the perimeter, I'll send up a prayer you get your brain dislodged from your ass sometime before the next millennium."

"Yeah, you do that, Hawke. And mind your own business. *Fuck.*"

Theo sucked in air and stayed where he was for a good five minutes after Hawke took off. He rolled the beer can along his forehead, fighting his temper, and wishing for a king-sized bottle of painkillers to soothe his aching head and the pain in his chewed-up hand. Damn.

He loved Melena and it was killing him.

Two minutes later, he barged through her bedroom door.

"Don't you knock?"

She rolled out of bed, tossed her head, and planted herself in front of him, fists on her hips. His fantasy Wonder Woman was alive and well, and spoiling for a fight. She was draped in a peach satin thing that clung to every curve, cinched her waist, and ended at the tops of her thighs. *Whoa, what happened to the sweat suit?*

"Theo, you can't just barge in here—"

With supreme effort, he tore his gaze away from her cleavage. "Here's the thing, Mel. I think you care about me and I sure as hell care about you. So if you want to hook up, I'm your man. And if you want to live together and take turns cooking and sorting laundry, I'm still your man. We'll divide the responsibilities fifty-fifty, straight down the middle."

"However, when it comes to dangerous situations, there will be no splitting the workload. I'm in charge, plain and simple, sugar. I'm not making a macho statement here; it's a question of survival, situations I have been trained for. I need you to trust that I'm the *only* one in our relationship capable of making those decisions for both of us. What's it going to be?"

She didn't respond at first, only squared her shoulders and licked her bottom lip, a quick flash of pink tongue. He waited her out, trying not to search for panty lines beneath her nightshirt.

Her breasts moved, her nipples rasping the gauzy fabric with every intake of her breath. The puckering buds begged for his mouth. He almost choked on his saliva.

Her intoxicating scent swirled around him, mysterious and sensuous. Theo moved to the window, threw it open and adjusted the front of his jeans before he ended up crippled. He turned back to face her.

Glossy blond hair wisped around her face in sexy spikes. Incredible blue eyes flashed at him beneath thick dark lashes. She stared down her straight little nose at him.

"I guess I could live with those conditions. But, I will kick your butt if you don't keep me up to speed when you're away with your team."

He barely recognized his own voice, which came out an octave too high. "Hell, sugar, I'm your man."

# Chapter 18

Theo leaned into her and tipped her chin with a finger. He pulled her up on her toes and into his arms, his lips met hers as he backed her toward the bed.

After that scorching kiss, Melena could hear herself breathing in short, excited bursts. Their hearts pounded together, chest to chest and beat for beat.

Easing her down on the quilt, Theo knelt over her, slowly sliding her nightshirt over her hips, almost as if he were opening a package. His hard ridge nudged her tummy as he breathed fire along her neck.

Frustrated at the pace he had chosen, she tossed the nightgown over her head and reached for the snap on his jeans. His lips slanted over hers again while she worked the zipper. He tightened his hold on her as he seemed to finally understand she needed him. His assault on her mouth quickened; her limbs weakened when his tongue slipped past her teeth and entwined with her own. Her feminine core clenched and unclenched. He tasted like liquid heat.

Pushing him to the bed, she slid to her knees in front of him and planted feather-light kisses across his chest, her arms wrapped around his neck, her body humming with physical need. He chucked his jeans and suited up in a condom from his wallet.

His hands smoothed up her ribcage to cup her breasts, his mouth zeroing in and suckling hard. Soft moans escaped her throat; each caress of his lips had her begging for more.

"Lay back," he said, easing her against the pillows. She wasn't prepared for what Theo did next. Shouldering her legs wide, his palms skimmed the curls protecting her mound. Fingers tracing along its edges, he opened her folds. His mouth followed, stroking her nub with a cadence that drove her wild. Sure. Slow. Steady. She clutched his hair and moaned, rocked on a building wave of climax.

"That's it, sugar." He blew across her curls, hands smoothing up her stomach to reclaim her breasts. "Let me enjoy you."

His lips touched down again, his tongue stroking her insides with powerful flicks. Her body shook as he drove her higher, over the edge. She climaxed on a bucking wave.

Without giving her time to regroup, he straightened, kept her legs on his shoulders, and drove himself into her with powerful thrusts. "Ah...Melena..."

He sent her higher, loved her as she'd never been loved before—with strength, but also a need to please that touched her soul. He gave, yet wasn't afraid to take when she later brought him into her mouth.

They were perfect together on every level. The sex was mind-blowing, the love flowing between them electrifying.

Sometime later Hawke knocked at the door. "Is everything okay in there?"

Theo looked down at her snuggled in his arms and a grin played across his lips.

"Oh, yeah. I'm just getting my brain out of my ass."

"Well, roger that."

THE TRIP TO THE LOCAL police station early the next morning wound Melena tight. Even if it went well, she didn't want to talk about Campo and the attacks on her. Or remember finding his body. All she wanted to do was forget. Forget everything, including her newly discovered biological father whom she couldn't talk about with the police.

There was also the cartel, another off-limits subject. The interview would be difficult if not impossible for her to pull off. She guessed the drama classes she had taken as a lark back at the university were about to come into play. The last thing she needed right now was closer scrutiny from the cops.

She understood the urgency; Theo hadn't waited for the sergeant to come to her for obvious reasons. If Vincelli's boys showed up at the house while the cops were there it would be a catastrophe. People might die. He and his team could handle the cartel far more efficiently without police involvement. So, she'd let Theo lead her to the precinct, knees knocking as she prayed for divine intervention.

The building on the street corner resembled a small alpine lodge, a wooden structure with lots of glass overlooking the town square. It was almost welcoming. Still, she imagined the grilling that would take place once she passed through the door.

Giving her statement to the sergeant would be like skating on thin ice. It was a question of half truths. How much to tell him and what she needed to leave out.

Slowing her pace, she stopped to stare at the window display of a gift boutique. She'd be a few minutes late for her meeting if she lingered, but badly needed to get herself under control.

Theo wrapped an arm around her shoulders and kissed her cheek. "I'm not asking you to lie, exactly. But we have to end this thing with the cartel. If the cops get involved, it'll only drag it out. Vincelli will lay low for a while, biding his time until the police aren't around anymore to protect you. That will leave you as fair game in his eyes."

She hugged his waist and leaned into him, knowing she trusted Theo with her life. If she did as he asked, he would keep her safe when no one else could.

"Sully said the RCMP would get involved if the police find out about Vincelli. They'd put me in Witness Protection and I'd have to disappear for the rest of my life...or at least until this goes to trial."

He cupped her face and tipped her chin, the look in his eyes fierce. "This will never see the inside of a courtroom, Mel. We can't prove Vincelli's involvement with Campo and the attacks on you. Even if your father testifies to the cartel's money laundering and illegal activities, those crimes took place in the U.S."

"Right. If I want to keep on breathing, I can't talk about Vincelli or my father." Her tummy cramped with a stab of fear. She flinched and almost doubled over.

Theo guessed what had happened, splayed his hand over her abdomen, and rubbed in gentle circles. The pain soon disappeared with the caress of his fingers, replaced by the warmth of his touch. Another few minutes and she forgot her fear. Courage bubbled inside her with the knowledge her plan could work. She grabbed Theo's hand. "I'm okay now. Come with me while I freshen up."

Melena rounded the corner into an alley, undid the top three buttons of her white blouse and opened the collar as wide as it would go. She winked at Theo, rolled her tight red skirt up several inches at the waist, pulled a mirror and lipstick from her makeup kit and rouged her lips, glossy cherry.

After fluffing her spiked hair, she reached into her oversized handbag and exchanged her serviceable espadrilles for the four-inch scarlet heels she'd dragged from her suitcase that morning. She only wore them for dressy events, called them her hooker shoes.

Theo raised his eyebrows and gawked. He seemed to be working enough spit into his mouth to say something. "What the heck you doing, sugar?"

"What does it look like I'm doing?" She laughed, not at him, but at the fact she was starting to enjoy herself. "I'm pulling a Marilyn Monroe."

"You're doing wha...?"

"Trust me on this. Just follow my lead."

Melena sashayed across the town square as if her hips were double jointed. She savored the role she played. If the sergeant watched her from behind the windows of the cop shop, she hoped he was drooling. Pushing through the door with Theo on her heels, she paused and cocked a hip.

The sergeant was at her elbow in an instant. He was tall and thin with a pencil moustache, and eyes that already devoured her cleavage.

"Mademoiselle Salera? I've been expecting you. Sergeant Louis Dupré at your service."

"I'm so pleased to meet you, Sergeant," she breathed. "This is my lawyer, Theo Sauvage."

His gaze flicked briefly over Theo with disdain, resettled again on her breasts. "Please, call me Louis. And there's no need for you to have legal representation. Asking you a few questions about Monsieur Campo is only a formality. Shall we go into my office?"

Melena agreed and passed in front of him, giving him the full benefit of her backside in the tight skirt. She strutted her way to the corner office with his nameplate on the door, Theo following.

Once inside, the sergeant closed the door and motioned to chairs facing his desk. Melena settled herself, hiking her skirt as far as it would go as she crossed her legs. The sergeant's gaze alternated between the cleft of her blouse and the exposed skin of her thighs.

"Can I get you anything? Coffee, tea, a soft drink?"

"Thank you, but I'd prefer to get the questions over with." She closed her eyes, placed a hand against her heart. "I was so terrified of Campo, Louis. I still get palpitations thinking about him."

The sergeant leaned forward in his chair. "There is no need to be afraid anymore, mademoiselle. The scum is dead, no doubt killed by the family of some other unsuspecting woman he forced himself on."

A small cry escaped her. Dupré came out of his chair and skirted his desk to bend over her with concern. She chanced a quick peek at Theo. Crossing his eyes, he snorted then masked it with a cough. A pointy toe of her shoe shot out and jabbed him in the shin while the sergeant focused on her cleavage.

"I don't want to cause you any distress." The sergeant took her hand. She wanted to gag, but pressed her fingers more firmly into his. "I know Campo attacked you on two different occasions. I was at your cottage with the coroner when we took the bodies away of his accomplices. No one blames you for what happened, mademoiselle. But I need to know how you met Campo. What caused him to come after you?"

A tear rolled down her cheek. She wiped it away with her free hand, the other still clinging to the sergeant's. "It was a nightmare, Louis. He accosted me at the boat landing when I first arrived at Silver Lake. I was alone in the parking lot. He...he put his hands on me."

Dupré clucked his tongue in sympathy. "It must have been a horrible experience for you. Needless to say, you spurned his advances."

"Yes...yes I did. And somehow I managed to get away." Another tear fell, this time on the sergeant's knuckles. Another heave of her breasts as she forced her lips to tremble. "I don't remember the details. Just the thought of that animal groping me still gives me nightmares."

"I completely understand." The sergeant patted her shoulder, stood up, and adjusted his belt. "This is obviously a case of ego, Mademoiselle. You spurned Campo's advances and he didn't like it. He must have followed you down the lake, discovered where you live, and then came back with his gang to force himself on you."

"You think that's what happened, Louis?" She dug deep for an appropriate shuddering gasp. And felt guilty for deceiving the sergeant. "Believe me; I never encouraged Campo's advances in any way."

"Yes, that's clear to me now." Dupré fondled his moustache, risking another glance at her exposed skin.

"I say this in only the most professional of terms, but you are a very desirable woman. The man was clearly a serial rapist and he wanted you to be his next victim. I suspected as much. But then you discovered his body. I knew you weren't responsible for his death, but I had to follow procedure. Can you forgive me, mademoiselle?"

"Why of course, Louis. You were the man in charge of the investigation. I expected nothing less from you than a thorough examination of all the facts. It's such a relief to me to know I have you to thank for such excellent police work."

"I am happy to serve you, mademoiselle, should you ever need my assistance. But, as far as I'm concerned you were not involved in the matter of Campo's death. The subject is officially closed."

COLD METAL BIT INTO Theo's hand as he opened the door for Melena. Head held high, she stepped out of the police station, hips swaying, one hand on her waist while her purse swung from the other. She paused at the bottom of the stairs and, sensing she was slowing down, Theo glanced sideways and gave her a nudge.

"Don't let up now, sugar. Keep the show going. Sergeant Dupré's in the window watching you go. We don't want him to know your 'Marilyn Monroe' was all an act now, do we?"

Waiting until they had turned the corner, Melena elbowed him in the ribs. "Quit making fun of me. My little *show* got us out of there, didn't it?"

"I was paying you a compliment."

Melena drilled him with her cobalt baby blues.

"I'm serious." He cupped her elbow and swung her around to face him. Teetering on those deadly heels, she lost her balance as he tugged, coming up snug against him as he planted a kiss on her lips. "Thanks to you, he bought it hook, line and sinker. And babe, you looked so good doing it."

Melena rolled her eyes, the beginnings of a smile turning the corners of her mouth up. Jesus, she was delicious—and smart. He'd learned something from her today. Sometimes a soft approach worked better than the Special Ops ones in his playbook.

"You were spectacular with Dupré," he murmured against her mouth and, teasing her with the promise of his kiss, threw caution to the wind, admitting, "and I learned a valuable lesson from you in there."

"Really?" she hummed, letting him know how much she enjoyed his touch as her fingers played with the hair at the nape of his neck. "Let's hear it, Sparky."

"Well, I learned that a little subtlety goes a long way, even if it's coming from a working girl."

"Oh! Wait just a minute—"

"Yeah, the sergeant didn't know what hit him. You were his wet dream. And because of that, I didn't have to bruise my knuckles to make him understand the complexities of your situation. Hell, you were my fantasy today too. How did you know I have a thing for high class hookers?"

That did it. She hauled off and thwacked him in the chest with her purse. "You insufferable ass."

Theo grinned like an idiot and dug for his cell phone as it vibrated in the front pocket of his jeans. He hit the right hand button, putting it on speaker. "What's up?"

"Stella called," Sully said. "Someone was at the store asking a lot of questions about the setup at Sarah's place. She was vague with her answers, but said he went down to the pier and talked to some other folks. She managed to get a look at his ride. Judging by the rifle cases and equipment in the back of the SUV, Stella says he came loaded for bear."

Theo squeezed Melena's arm in reassurance, sensing she wanted to bolt. "This isn't hunting season."

"No. It looks like the big guns and our bigger fish have arrived," Sully agreed.

When Melena winced beside him, Theo laced his fingers with hers and held on. "It's a safe bet Vincelli's upped the ante, maybe offered a bonus. His crew is moving in."

"I'm at the docks. The SUV's gone. Get Melena back here so we can get her home."

"Ten minutes tops." Theo disconnected. "Ditch the hooker shoes, sugar. They'll pinch your toes and slow us down."

THEY CAME OUT OF THE mist at dawn the next morning riding jet-skis, a woman and two men. Theo knew they were coming before they had cleared the last bay. Sully saw them pass by his location and radioed ahead. Now Sully and Reece were following at a distance with Mic, Hunt and Ken Davidson racing from the other end of the lake to close ranks. These assholes weren't getting past them.

Theo ran for the bunkhouse with Melena still in her nightgown and heaved her into the crawl space. "Stay up there until I come for you and don't make a sound."

"Ugh, there are spiders up here. Big ones."

*Go figure*, he thought wryly. The woman had been assaulted, gone up against dangerous felons on three different occasions, tripped over a dead body, braved the thunderstorm, and survived a boating disaster. But, she couldn't stare down a measly spider without getting the heebie-jeebies?

He slammed the trap door on her petrified face and locked it. "I'm sorry but this isn't up for debate. Hey, better the spiders than a bullet to your brain. Don't move a muscle, Mel. I'll be back for you."

By the time he got back to the cabin, Hawke and Law were already in position. Sully's voice came over his headset. "They're on the island now, hiking across from the other side. The jet-skis are stashed in a cove and we're disabling them. We'll be behind them all the way, bro."

"Roger that." Theo could hear tree limbs cracking in the distant woods. "Jeez, these guys are klutzy as hell. I can hear them coming a mile off."

"Yeah, well this isn't exactly the streets of Las Vegas, but don't underestimate them. They're carrying some heavy artillery and they're pros."

Theo felt, rather than heard, someone creeping up behind him. He palmed his Glock, spun on a dime, and pointed the business end directly at...Melena's head. *Shit!* "How in God's name did you get out of the crawl space?"

"Climbed out the attic window and shimmied down a tree. I told you. There are spiders in there." She gaped around her bedroom as if seeing it for the first time. "What are those lumps in my bed? Are those supposed to be us sleeping? Please, let me help you...give me one of your guns."

*Shit. Shit. Shit.* Melena thought she was Annie Oakley. Theo heard the kitchen door snick open and knew they had run out of time. He hissed in her ear. "You are *not* playing with guns today. Get in the bedroom closet and stay low. I want you to keep very still and very quiet. If things get rough, I need to know where you are. Got it?"

"Yes." She brought his hand to her lips and kissed it along the puffy wound where she had bitten him. Then she moved silently into the small space. Theo backed in behind her.

"I love you, Theo," she whispered. "Please, stay safe."

*She loved him. She actually loved him.* There wasn't time to say the things he wanted to say, the things he needed her to hear. Later. It would have to be later.

He cracked the door open an inch and waited for the show to start. It wasn't much of a wait. He saw the gun before he saw the arm it belonged to, the woman's arm. She was a large-boned, big-breasted brunette with thick wrists, manly features and murder on her mind.

Her two sidekicks slid into view, wise guys depicting the mob stereotype right down to their noses flattened in some bar-room brawl, greased-back hair and flashy gold chains hanging from thick, stubby necks. Both of them were mid-thirties with muscles turning to flab and paunchy guts. All of them wore wetsuits, maybe because of the ride on the jet-skis or maybe to prevent blood from spattering their clothing. They formed a line at the foot of the bed. Locked and loaded.

# Chapter 19

It was so dark in the closet, only the barest sliver of light reached Melena from the crack in the door. She inched closer to the back wall, the floorboards creaking beneath her bare feet. Was the noise too loud? Was the death squad turning toward the closet at this very moment to open fire?

Theo's hand gripped her hip, cautioning her to silence. Something else touched her shoulder. She flinched and almost screamed. Her grandmother's bathrobe rocked on its hanger, the faint scent of Lily of the Valley reaching her nose. Heart hammering, Melena's fingers brushed the bathrobe, half believing her grandmother was there in the closet with her, trying to ease her fears.

Her palms sweated at the thought of the animals standing on the other side of the door. Terror gripped her, but oddly not for herself. Theo stood between her and the thugs, acting as a human shield. He would die before he would let anything happen to her. And surely those lumps in her bed weren't Hawke and Law? No, she reasoned, that made no sense at all. They must be hiding somewhere.

At the woman's sharp command, the goon squad opened fire on the bed. Melena covered her ears with her hands and squeezed her eyes tightly shut. If the decoys in her bed had been human, they would already be dead. Meanwhile, she hid in the closet like a damn coward. Suddenly, everything went very still, the absolute silence ringing in her ears. Nothing moved but the smoke and mattress stuffing floating through the air. Melena inhaled the smell of cordite and almost choked on it.

One minute Theo was in front of her. The next he was gone. Blinded and panicked, Melena felt for the door handle and pushed. Nothing happened. He'd locked her in. *Theo!*

Furniture toppled, glass smashed. Painful grunts and curses surrounded her. It sounded like guns hitting the floor. She held her breath, leaned against the door. Theo opened it. She fell through and collapsed in a heap.

"Mel? Are you all right?"

Theo and Law stood directly between her and Vincelli's goons, their backs to her, their Glocks aimed steadily at three heads. Hawke dropped through the skylight and gathered up the weapons, tossing them on the bed. Another few minutes and the perpetrators were searched, bound at the wrists and ankles, and laying face-down on the floor.

Theo turned to her and squatted to her level, balanced on his heels to surround her with his warmth. He touched his forehead to hers. "The worst is over now. But, stay with me until Sully gets here with the others. I don't want you out of my sight until I have an update on this situation."

"Where do you think I'm going to go?" She wanted to burrow under his skin and stay there. Warm. Safe. Did he really think she was going to dash off by herself to prepare hors d'oeuvres in the kitchen after seeing those bullets flying around?

"With you I never know." He clamped a hand around her arm, hauled her off the floor, and guided her out of the room. "God, you just don't know when to quit. Every time I think you're safely out of harm's reach, you are not where you're supposed to be. You just scared another ten years off my life. Hell, sugar, even for a cat you would be running out of lives right about now."

"I'll pay attention next time, okay?" Her smile was shaky, her voice warbled, and tears clouded her vision. "I wasn't sure...I thought Law and Hawke might actually be in my bed. I thought they could be d-dead."

"Yo, Mel, this was a walk in the park for us. We're all fine here," Hawke called out behind them. He and Law were scraping their adversaries off the floor and dragging them to the living room.

"Yeah. The only damage done is to a couple of bedrolls and your mattress," Law offered. "I don't think you'll be using those again but they're all replaceable."

THEO PIVOTED AS SULLY and the others came through the main door of the house. "Thanks for the heads up on our visitors."

"Our pleasure, bro."

"Holy shit!" Ken exclaimed as he viewed the prisoners on the floor. "Do you know who this is? You've just captured the mother lode, Theo. This is Angelo's only child, Tony Vincelli."

Theo eyed the men on the floor. They both glared up at him sullenly. "Which one of these assholes is Tony?"

"Not them. Her." Ken pointed a finger in the woman's direction. "That's Antoinette Vincelli, man. She flew with me enough times that I'd know her anywhere. Hey, Antoinette, what are you doing here?"

"It's Tony," she snapped. "It's always been Tony. Get it straight."

"Well, well." Theo's grin split from ear to ear. "Will some of you guys take these gentlemen out to the bunkhouse and make them comfortable? And if they so much as twitch, shoot off their kneecaps."

By the time Reece, Hunt and Law moved to drag the men outside, Micah and Hawke had Tony Vincelli off the floor and tied to a chair in the dining room. Theo dragged another chair over to hers and straddled it backward. Silently, he gave the woman credit. She didn't so much as flinch.

Tony eyed Ken and Melena warily before speaking. "I'm sorry, Ken. I always liked you and I tried to talk my father out of this stupid vendetta. But, he wouldn't listen."

Ken crouched down close to her and placed a hand on her arm. "I never thought of you as the killing type. If I remember correctly, you went off to Harvard to get your business degree. You told me you had dreams of running the family's businesses legitimately. What happened?"

"I've been doing just that, successfully running the casinos and our other interests within the letter of the law. Until my father discovered you were still alive and gave me the ultimatum of either eliminating you and your daughter or being kicked out of the cartel."

"Lady, that's some change in job descriptions." Theo scowled. "I guess the fruit doesn't fall far from the tree. Daddy threatens to take away your pay check, so you offer to go out and slaughter a few people to keep your job? Talk about multi-tasking."

"You don't understand!" She lashed back. "My father is a selfish, brutal man. He doesn't care about the repercussions of his decisions on the family. He cares about vengeance, wants Ken and his daughter killed and that's the end of it. I would be dead, too, if I'd gone against him."

"My heart bleeds for you. Listen to me, very carefully." Theo's voice turned deadly. He pointed to Melena, standing a little away from him. "That woman is *not* going to be harmed in any way by you, your father or the cartel. And that includes the members of her family and anyone else she holds dear. I don't care what your father wants. If he persists in this vendetta, I will take you all out. I'll destroy everyone in my path if that's what it takes to keep her breathing."

"I'm with you all the way on this," Sully added coldly. "The whole team is behind you, one hundred percent."

"You know, maybe the Vincellis don't understand who they're playing with," Micah drawled. "Maybe you should explain the facts of life to Antoinette here."

"Good idea, Mic," Hawke said. "Maybe Tony hasn't factored in the army at your disposal—an army that makes the cartel's goon squad look like a bunch of pansies."

Theo nodded to his brother and his friends, the strength of their allegiance filling his chest. "See, Tony, if you kill any of us, others will keep on coming. We're highly skilled men, trained to kill, to eliminate a target and leave no evidence behind. We can hurt you in ways that would make even your old man blanch. Believe me when I say—all of you will die screaming."

"And just for the record, we have limitless firepower and ways of flying under the radar, even to Las Vegas. It's what we *do*, Tony. It's *who* we are. If I make good on my promise, the cartel won't know what hit them until it's far too late. So, what's it going to be?"

Hopefully Tony knew enough about his breed to know he wasn't bluffing. Theo needed little Miss Cartel to understand. Love for Melena made him lethal. The worst sort of adversary.

"All right. I need to make a phone call."

Theo dialed the number she gave him, hit speaker phone and held the cell up to her face. "Papa? I'm in trouble."

"What the hell happened?" Angelo Vincelli's voice boomed on the other end of the line. "Did you handle the problem?"

"No. Davidson and his daughter had protection and they set a trap for us. We're being held hostage."

"Christ. I raised you to be smarter than that. Can't you do anything right? No wonder I wanted a son to run the business."

"Did you hear anything your daughter just said?" Theo snarled. "Be on the next commercial flight out of Las Vegas for Montreal. And I'm warning you, you're being watched, so don't do anything stupid. Come alone or your daughter dies. You'll be met at the airport."

Theo disconnected the call as his eyes cut to Melena, still standing there trembling in an oversized sleep shirt. She looked as if a stiff breeze would knock her flat. He rose from his chair, looped an arm around her waist, and tugged her outside and out of earshot.

"Are you doing okay?"

"Oh, sure. I'm just terrific." She ran shaking fingers through her hair then turned her pale, upturned face to his. "You can't seriously be thinking about killing those people? This is a nightmare. Please, Theo, don't do this because of me."

"Hey, it's only a bluff." He grabbed her hand, kissed each of her knuckles, and linked them with his, strolling with her slowly along the path surrounding the cabin.

"Trust me on this, sugar. A show of force is the only way to make the cartel back off and leave you in peace. I've dealt with bullies like Vincelli for most of my life. Violence is the only language he understands."

"But, what if he doesn't listen? What if he doesn't back down?"

"He'll be as good as dead." Theo hated to say it, didn't enjoy the violence he'd spent a lifetime committing for his country, but he would kill Angelo Vincelli in a heartbeat for Melena. There was little choice. Melena was an innocent, while the Vincellis were murderous scum having no respect for human life. Besides, he loved her beyond reason and he would do what was necessary to keep her in his future. "You said you loved me, back there, before the bullets started flying. Well, I love you, too. And I'm asking you to trust me."

She gazed into his eyes. "You love me?"

"Yeah, sugar...with all my heart. I know this isn't the best time to tell you. But, I'm counting on us having a long life together. The cartel doesn't enter into my plans. I want you in one piece so you can marry me, Mel."

"Well, well, isn't this a touching scene?" A man stepped away from the shadows of a stand of timber, his gun aimed directly at Melena. He pulled her in close to him before Theo could block the move, the gun snugged neatly beneath her chin. A woman stood beside him, a shapely blonde with a rifle aimed at Theo's chest. "Drop your weapon."

Theo did as he was told, never taking his eyes off the man with the gun aimed at Melena's head.

"That was a very poignant marriage proposal, by the way. Too bad the lady won't be around long enough to take you up on your offer. Neither will you, for that matter."

Theo surveyed the scene, wondering where the hell Sully and the others were. They had to know what was going on. They could hear everything that transpired through his headset and would be looking for ways to take down these two.

Why hadn't anyone seen them arrive? The man was bulky and bullish. Hard to miss. He was also edging toward his twilight years, way too old to be a hit man. "Who are you? What do you want?"

The man's pinkie ring caught the sunlight for an instant. Theo made out the diamond studded 'V' embedded in black onyx and edged with gold, and he knew.

Angelo Vincelli barked out a laugh. "Ah, I see you've already made the connection. Aren't satellite phones the most amazing inventions? I can take a call anywhere in the world, and in this case; I was over in the next bay, ready to clean up after my highly incompetent daughter."

Theo's muscles bunched, waiting to spring, looking for an opening if Vincelli would only let his guard down and move the gun a fraction of an inch away from Melena's temple. He could kill him with one well-placed kick, but not before the man shot her dead. Or a bullet from the blonde's rifle tore through his own heart. "Hurt her and you die."

Vincelli yanked on Mel's hair, wrenching a cry from her. Her eyes widened with fear and locked on Theo. "Leave me, Theo. Save yourself!"

Angelo threw back his head and roared at the thought, while the woman beside him just smirked. He nodded to Theo. "Tell your men inside to drop their weapons and get my daughter and Kenny out here. Now!"

Theo issued the command through his mike, knowing full well his men wouldn't surrender in a hostage situation, knowing that all hell was about to break loose. He needed to get Melena safely out of the line of fire before that happened.

Unfortunately, he couldn't see how he was going to do it. Things were moving too fast. Tony Vincelli had already cleared the door with Ken walking close behind her.

Angelo hailed his daughter with a barrage of insults. "Ya see, Tony, this is how your old man takes care of business. You screwed up, as usual, which proves you'll never run the cartel. Get the hell over here."

"I'm coming, Papa." She went meekly toward them, trembling at the sight of her father, head down, feet shuffling. Theo watched her move, realizing her body language was off. Maybe the meek little mouse wasn't meek at all.

As she walked by the pilot, something dropped into her palm. If Theo hadn't eyeballed her so closely, he would have missed the exchange. In a flash, Tony lifted her arm and plunged a syringe into the side of her father's neck. "Bye, Papa."

"Tony...what have you done?" She twisted the gun from Angelo's hand as he slumped to the ground, clawing at his throat and gasping for air. His skin was breaking out in hives, his face swelling, his voice barely an audible rasp. "Dottie...help...epinephrine..."

The other woman winked, lowered her weapon, and captured Tony in a lover's embrace while Angelo writhed at their feet.

Tony watched her father dispassionately, then sidestepped around him, took Melena by an arm, and guided her toward Theo. She shrugged as she stopped in front of him.

"Bee venom. My father is deathly allergic. I knew he wouldn't be far away, thanks to Dottie. That he wouldn't trust me to get this job done. I was counting on it and came prepared. My father's reign of terror has to end for all of us. I was just waiting for the right opportunity."

"You retired Campo as well?" Theo had a hunch he knew the answer before he asked the question.

She grinned. "He won't bother you again."

"Tony," Ken said, aghast, as the others poured from the cottage and bunkhouse to gather around the fallen man. "You're killing your own father. Isn't there some other way to end this?"

"He's an animal, Ken, incapable of any empathy or remorse. That's what I'm killing. I wish things could be different."

Another shrug. "By the way, I want you to meet my new pilot, Dottie."

The other woman and Ken shook hands, Ken pumping her fingers automatically while seemingly in a daze. Theo studied Tony Vincelli closely as he picked up his Glock and clamped Melena tightly to his side, grateful for the chance to hold her again. Understanding for Tony's actions sparked in some black corner of his soul.

She was cleaning house. The cartel could now move forward in her very capable hands and the old ways of doing business were finally over. "What do you want us to do?"

"Let Rico and Frankie go, so they can carry my father to the plane."

She glanced from Theo to Sully and the other men on his team. "You see, we also have ways of flying under the radar. I want my father found in the garden on his estate. Our *family* doctor will sign the death certificate for his tragic, but accidental, death."

She held out her hand and Theo grasped it. "It's over between us. It ends here. Ken can return to his life. He and his daughter don't have to worry about the Vincelli cartel ever again. I give you my word. Our business with you has been satisfactorily concluded."

"What about the money I owed your father?" Ken asked.

"Consider it hazard pay. I always liked you. You cared about my dreams for the business when no one else would listen. That meant a lot to me. Besides, my father hired Campo to kill your mother. He shouldn't have done that. Now he's paying the price. That makes us even."

Tony turned to Melena. "I'm sorry this had to happen to you. Take care of your man and have a good life together. You know, without him and your father, you wouldn't be alive now. I would have carried through on Papa's wishes. They prevented me from doing that."

Theo and Melena fell in behind as the procession wound its way down to the dock. After Dottie was ferried to their plane moored in the next bay, she taxied it back to their location. Vincelli's barely twitching body was loaded in the cargo hold by Tony's men.

"Pack him in ice." Tony spoke as if she was talking about the morning's catch after deep sea fishing. When it was her turn to board, she swung around in the doorway and waved a salute. "If you ever get to Vegas be sure to look me up. I can promise you safe passage in my neck of the woods."

*Sure, in about a hundred gazillion years,* Theo thought.

# Epilogue

"Sarah's case is officially closed," Theo told Melena as they lay in the hammock together under the stars. Dood was stretched out beneath the hammock in his doggie bed. "Sully managed to convince the sergeant that it was Campo who killed Sarah, with an eye on getting her money. He even convinced him that's why Campo came after you."

"Really? And just how did he explain away Campo's death?"

"The usual. The traditional falling out among thieves. Sully can be very persuasive when he uses his cop demeanor. He suggested a fourth man must have been involved but got away."

Melena reached in the ice bucket and topped off their champagne flutes. "Uh-huh. I guess that's better than trying to explain away the truth. No one would believe us anyway."

Theo's friends had packed up and left that morning, after a lot of grateful tears and hugs on her part. Hawke was moving on to Houston to oversee Joelle's protection. Something about a fan stalking her.

Reece 'Rocket' Morgan had hightailed it out of there like a house on fire after receiving a phone call.

Melena had a feeling they would be hearing a lot more from Reece and Hawke in the near future.

She hadn't spoken with her parents since this whole thing had begun, had yet to confront them about keeping her adoption a secret. And she hadn't decided if she wanted to pursue a relationship with Ken Davidson or find out more about her mother's side of the family in Montreal.

These things required a great deal of thought and would have to wait for another day. Still, she had a hunch she'd move forward in both those areas. For now, she was happy to be alive and in the arms of the man she loved.

Finally, she and Theo were alone. She turned on her side and snuggled against him. "Well, I guess we'd better get busy."

"There's nothing to do. What do you mean?"

"Breeana and Sully are leaving for San Antonio tomorrow with your parents. Your mom wants to take Breeana shopping for her wedding dress. That means Cody and Pierre will be moving in with us for a few days. And *that* means separate bedrooms."

"Oh, brother." Theo brushed a kiss across her forehead and groaned softly. "I don't suppose we could cheat a little? Maybe send the boys to the store at the landing for milk? I'm pretty sure that's what my parents did when I was a kid. The fridge was always full of milk, but Joelle, Sully, and I were sent for more at least once a day. It seems to me we needed a lot of bread too. Sometimes we would be sent back to the store in the afternoon."

"Oh, yes." Mel nuzzled his neck and nipped at his ear, inhaling his wonderful scent and smiling with anticipation. "We're going to need milk. Lots and lots of milk. And bread!"

Theo chuckled softly and gave her a firm squeeze. "I love you."

"Really? Then how about showing me?"

"Happy to oblige, sugar. Happy to oblige."

THANK YOU FOR READING this book. I hope you enjoyed it but even if you didn't, please take a few moments to go back online where you purchased it and leave an honest review. Authors absolutely depend on reviews to know how readers feel about their books and series. Thank you, it's appreciated.

For a free book, please hop over to my website at https://www.kallielane.com

# A word about the author...

This is me in a nutshell. I was raised in Montreal and still have a home there, although most of my thriller and suspense novels come alive in my writing den, at a small cottage I love in the mountains. I guess I've always been a country girl at heart.

My constant companions these days are a Rottweiler, an American Bully, and a cat rescue. I'm widowed and have two adult sons who, I'm sure, worry about what trouble I'm getting into on a daily basis. Case in point; I've managed to break a few bones and dislocate others over the last few years when 'playing' with my dogs. While they are advanced obedience trained and a pleasure to have, I sometimes roughhouse with them a little too much. I also enjoy taking the boat out in the wee hours of the morning to see the stars and the night sky at the cottage. But, yes, I always have my cell phone handy. I'm sure if I didn't answer, someone would call 9-1-1.

I worked in the pharmaceutical and biotech industries for several years, and now I can finally enjoy writing as my real job, which I've dreamt about doing since I was a teenager. Wowzers! How lucky can a girl be? My spare time is shared with family and friends, including writer friends, and I work out to keep myself in shape, rather than dog wrestling! I'm an avid reader and spend more time with a book or tablet in my hands than watching television. Oh, I also like to travel, whether it's for business or pleasure, but I'm mostly found at the keyboard fulfilling my passion for writing.

I love to hear from readers, so please drop me an email at kallie_lane@ymail.com and I promise I'll message back. Lastly, I hope you enjoyed what you read. I would love it if you would leave a review where you purchased this book. It matters to me (and all authors) how you feel about our stories. Wishing you the very best!

To learn more about Kallie, visit her website at **https://www.kallielane.com** or follow her on Facebook at **http://www.facebook.com/KallieLaneAuthor**

Here's a sneak peek at book 3 in the Shadow Soldiers Suspense series, available wherever you purchased previous books in the series...

# Reckless Abandon

## Chapter 1

The sun blazed overhead as Billie Bradshaw lay sprawled in the dirt, waiting to die. Cold and trembling, agonizing pain shooting through her head, she felt a drip along the base of her skull. She didn't move. Scarcely breathed and didn't open her eyes. Her mind wasn't working right. She didn't know how she'd gotten there. Yet, every instinct she possessed warned her to play dead.

Time ticked by, how much she couldn't tell before she recognized the whine of engines coming over the hill into the valley. Cracking her eyelids, she saw pickups with the *Circle B* insignia pull up and screech to a halt. Her father leapt from the first cab and raced toward her.

"Billie! Christ, we heard a shot!"

*What?*

He slid to his knees beside her, his body blocking the sun as he cupped her face in his hands. Searching his eyes, her escalating terror lessened a notch. Her dad would keep her safe, make sense of what had happened to her. Carefully, she tested her fingers and toes. They responded okay, she felt them move. She tried to speak but no sound came out. *What happened to my voice?*

"Hang on, love. Help's coming."

Ranch hands circled her, kicking up dust with their boots. Someone shouted loud enough to shatter her eardrums. "Keep your eyes on the hills. Shoot anything that moves!"

Sure, this was Grizzly country, but Billie surmised they weren't worried about bears. She turned her head, a big mistake, and almost fainted from the pain drilling her skull. Her father bunched his jacket into a pillow, lifted her head to slide it beneath her. More pain.

His phone rang. She listened to him yell at someone at the emergency clinic in Hereford before ending the call. "Damn ambulance broke an axle at the turnoff from the highway. A medevac team's on its way."

A few minutes later, she heard the sound of a helicopter clearing the treetops. She breathed in slowly, held tight to her father's hand, and watched it touch down beside the pickups. More dust. More men rushing at her. They wore flight suits, carried a stretcher and—*thank you, God!*—medical supplies.

They slid a board under her and strapped her to it, attached a neck brace and lifted her onto a stretcher. What could only be blood dripped on the board from her head. *Plop, plop,* so much of it...she hated its coppery scent. A man applied pressure behind her ear, began wrapping her head in bandages. She felt woozy again and fought to stay conscious. He asked her questions she mostly understood but couldn't seem to answer. *Why can't I speak? Shock, maybe?*

He was talking, always talking to her.

"How many fingers am I holding up, ma'am?" She held up three fingers.

"Can you squeeze my hand? Wiggle your toes and move your arms?"

She continued to do what he asked. *Now clam up, buddy, and give me some major drugs for this pain.*

Someone else pumped up her arm with a pressure cuff, used a stethoscope to listen to her heartbeat. If only her stupid voice would work, she could tell him her pulse roared through her head like a sonic boom. No need for the stethoscope to get a reading.

A third man hung an IV bag from a metal pole attached to the gurney, its contents dripping through a shunt into her arm. *Whatever you're feeding me, it's not pain meds. My head feels like it's going to explode.*

She coughed, choking on dust. An oxygen mask was placed over her nose.

Her father talked with the medevac team. He wanted a seat on the 'bus' that would airlift her to the hospital. Squeezing her eyes shut, she tried to ignore all of them. *Can't you leave me alone? You've already patched me up.*

"Wake up. Don't go to sleep." A hand tapped her cheek.

"Open your eyes. That's it." Fighting the void of darkness, she lifted her eyelids. Her father's face swam into view; strong, reticent, tense. The pulse at his throat pounded with concern. "Don't worry, darlin'. You're going to be fine. No more accidents."

*Accidents? I don't remember...*

As she was transferred to the chopper, her father spoke softly to their foreman. "Make the call. Get Rocket here. Now."

*What? No! No! Don't call him. Don't...*

The helicopter door clicked shut. Billie stretched out her fingers to clutch her father's sleeve. She moaned, trying to get the words out.

"Shh, I know what you're thinking, but you need Rocket. He's the only one I trust to protect you. He'll come. I know he will."

*I don't want him. This has nothing to do with that jerk. Don't call him!*

The torque of rotor blades and radio noise ended their one-way conversation. She was airborne, heading for the hospital. Her world began to fade from the pain not long into the flight, the seductive pull of unconsciousness blanketing her like a shroud.

REECE 'ROCKET' MORGAN sat on a barstool at *Charlie's*, a resto-bar high in the Laurentian mountains near Silver Lake in Quebec. Life was good, the team celebrating the safe rescue of Theo's lady from some very bad dudes. The fact a couple of good looking females had latched onto him like lint when he'd walked into the bar didn't hurt. Work was done. They wouldn't pile in the chopper for another few hours to head out. He had more than enough time to get to know the women, kick back, and relax.

"Reece, your phone's ringing," Sully, his Commanding Officer, bellowed from the table where some of the crew sat.

"Take a message." Reece kept his focus on the ladies. Seemed they had a thing for military guys. *Hoo-rah.*

"Guy called Pike says it's an emergency."

Reece pulled a hand down his face and groaned. Pike Williams, foreman of the *Circle B* ranch. A voice from his past, he'd taken him under his wing when Reece was nothing but a teenage punk. He owed him, and he'd take his call.

Walking to the table, he grabbed up his phone. "Pike? What's up, buddy?"

"Your girl's in trouble. You'd better get here quick."

"She's not my girl. And she's not my problem. Let her daddy handle whatever trouble she's in."

"She needs *you*, boy. Charley Bradshaw's the one who asked me to contact you. Didn't think you'd come if he called himself. She's in a passel of shit, that's for sure."

Reece laughed aloud at the remark. Billie was the only woman he knew who could bathe in crap and come out smelling like a margarita. "She must be for her old man to want me there. Last time I saw him he threatened to throw me in jail."

"Well, you sure can't blame him for that, Rocket. You shouldn't'a been diddling his little girl. Still, Charley's willing to let bygones be bygones. He's followed your military career—says you're the only one he trusts to help her now."

Pike was right about one thing. Billie Bradshaw had been underage when he'd slept with her. On his eighteenth birthday, they'd been caught in the back of his rusty pick-up behind the barn. That's when her father had threatened to charge him with statutory rape unless he zipped his pants, packed up his gear, and cleared out for good.

Tough call—go to jail or leave Billie. Reece had opted for door number two. Joined the military and never looked back. It still pissed him off he'd been booted to the curb with no chance to explain himself, although he'd deserved it. Hell, if the situation was reversed and he had a sixteen-year-old daughter? But, that was a lifetime ago.

*I'm not that dumb ass bastard anymore. And I don't need to prove myself to the Bradshaws.*

"Forget it, Pike. I'm not taking the bait. I cared about Billie. She obviously didn't feel the same way about me or she wouldn't have let her father ride me out of town on a rail."

"You cared for her, Rocket? Then why didn't you use protection instead of getting her pregnant?"

*Mother of God.* They'd only had sex one time. The news stunned him. He willed spit into his mouth to loosen his tongue. "Goddamn. Why am I only hearing about this now?"

"She wouldn't let me tell you, son." There was a pause on the other end of the line. Reece could hear Pike adding a chaw of tobacco to the inside of his cheek. "Besides, there's nothing to tell. She lost the baby four months into the pregnancy. Fell on a trail ride. Hit a rock and miscarried...nearly bled to death herself."

*Jesus, Jesus, Jesus.* Reece doubled over to catch his breath. He hadn't used a condom, hadn't protected Billie. "You're ten years too late. There's nothing I can do to make this right."

"Now you listen to me, or are you still just some snot-nosed kid who thinks he can take on the world with his fists? Come home, Rocket, and help her. I'm begging here. She won't make it without you, s-son, no matter how stubborn and t-tough she thinks she is."

Reece fought to level his breathing. Pike's voice had warbled, something he'd never heard before from the tough-as-nails foreman. Uneasiness gripped him. "What kind of trouble is she in?"

"Someone tried to kill her. I think they've tried before, but she won't listen to reason. She claims she's just been accident prone lately.

But, today they shot her upside the head. She was airlifted to the Foothills Medical Centre Trauma Unit for treatment."

Reece had no choice. He had to go. Not easy for a guy living off the grid. Harder because he still cared about her, and now he knew why she had never returned his calls or answered his letters. Jesus, a baby...loved and lost. He had caused so much pain in her life.

God help him, it was time to man up. "Give me the address."

Reece disconnected the call, turned to tell his teammates he had to boogie. Six pairs of eyes drilled him.

"Morgan, what's happening?" Law asked. "That call sounded serious."

"I have to get to the airport and charter a flight. A friend of mine was shot and needs my protection."

"You want help?" Micah rose from the table, looked ready to join him, no questions asked.

"Thanks. I'll let you know once I have more Intel." Reece slid the phone in his pocket and prepared to leave. "But I'll need a ride to the airport."

"Wheels up, guys." Hawke said. "Let's move."

A short time later, Reece stared out of the helicopter as it approached Montreal Trudeau airport. He needed a chance to clear his head and salvage his sanity. What he got instead was a high octane boost of adrenaline that clenched his jaw and vibrated clear to the soles of his metal-tipped boots.

One lousy phone call and his priorities had folded like a bad poker hand. Another call and he'd chartered a flight from Montreal to Calgary. A Bombardier Learjet 35A waited for him on the tarmac, revving its engines. Time was the enemy. He needed to reach Billie fast.

He also managed to reach his buddy with SARDAA—the Search and Rescue Dog Association of Alberta—to borrow a vehicle. He and Rizzo were tight. Ran into each other from time to time in stink hole situations such as natural disasters. Reece could count on him in a shit storm, the unlimited use of an SUV being the icing on the cake.

Less than five hours later, he was spinning out of Springbank Airport on a cloud of gravel and dust. If he put the pedal to the metal on the Cayenne, he'd make the hospital before nightfall. Hard to believe he burned rubber for the trauma unit. And her.

Billie Bradshaw—the only woman who still held the power to bring him to his knees.

*Why does she appeal to me?*

"Stupid question, man." He ran his hand over his face as he settled further into the seat.

Smart...beautiful...kind...shot out of his memory banks like a Christmas wish list. All the more reason he wanted to turn tail and run. Not from the potentially dangerous situation, but from the woman. Such was life. No time to dwell on it and even less time to lose. Billie needed him. And that said it all.

Cracking the window, he lit a cigarette—a habit he rarely indulged in anymore—shoved his aviator shades in place and blew out a stream of smoke. Better to die of cancer than go where he was headed now. There would be hell to pay.

BILLIE AWOKE TO DRUMS pounding her skull like a military tattoo. She was woozy and couldn't open her eyes. Her tongue was glued to the roof of her mouth, her throat was parched, and she couldn't reach or see to buzz the nurse's station for help.

She felt along the top of the nightstand until she bumped the plastic drinking cup with her fingers. Clutching it, she bobbled it to her lips. Her arm trembled and spasmed. The straw twirled. Freezing cold water sloshed over her hospital gown before a strong hand wrapped around hers and guided the straw to her mouth for a few quick swallows. "Want...more."

"Let's see how that stays down first."

The voice was deep, safe. *A male nurse?* He stripped off her soaked gown, dried her with a towel, and slipped another gown over her shoulders. The heaviness of a blanket soon cocooned her in warmth. Still, she couldn't hold back a whimper. "Hurts..."

Words became fuzzy, the doctor arguing with someone. "The dose is self-administering. All she has to do is push the button..."

"She can't push the button when she's too sick to open her eyes. Never mind, from now on I'll handle it for her."

"You can't stay here. You're not a relative."

Something started to flow through her veins; a magic elixir quieted the blasts going off in her head and further confused her mind. She drifted off for a while until the harsh voices startled her back to reality again.

"Not moving...phone her father...clear it...can't fend for herself...bodyguard."

*So tired. Can't stay awake. Can't make sense of what they're saying. Need to sleep.*

THE NEXT TIME BILLIE awakened she was able to lift her eyelids. Her gaze sharpened on a man standing in the doorway with his back to her. Very tall, he was narrow-hipped with faded jeans gloving his backside and long legs ending at a pair of scuffed boots. The black T-shirt he wore delineated powerful shoulders and bulging biceps. Corded sinews wrapped his muscular arms. Longish chestnut hair was secured at his nape by a strip of leather.

*Gorgeous.* She must be dreaming. Who was he? Some cowboy she met at a bar last night? *Impossible. Drunk or sober, I would remember sleeping with a man like him.*

He turned as if sensing her inspection. She instantly recognized those green, green eyes; his chiselled features; and a five o'clock shadow that seemed to be a permanent fixture on his jaw. Ten years older, he was a breathtaking version of the teenager she'd known. The teenager she'd loved. The teenager who'd scored and bolted, taking her heart along with him for the ride.

It wasn't a dream at all, but her worst nightmare. And why was a gun clipped to his belt?

She cleared her throat and found her voice. "You look like a hundred mile stretch of bad road, Rocket. What are you doing here?"

He cracked a smile displaying white, even teeth. Moving to the foot of the bed, the air around him hinted of sandalwood and peppermint. "It's nice to see you too, Billie. I see you're still styling your hair with a stun gun."

Actually, her hair didn't feel half bad when she ran her fingers through it in a self-conscious gesture. Oh, sure, it was long, wild, and curly, but at least it was brushed—except for where a mountain of bandages was taped behind her left ear. *What is that?*

"Not fair, Reece, like I've had time for the salon." She tried to hide her confusion by pulling herself higher in the bed. Starbursts flashed behind her eyes. Her vision tunnelled and her stomach heaved. "Whoa..."

"Be careful. There were complications—the bullet wound is infected."

*Bullet wound?*

She didn't move, waited for the dizziness to subside while she soaked up Reece's words. The ache in her head and her sense of helplessness said he was telling the truth.

She opened her eyes again, slowly refocused on pale cream walls, grimy windows with a view of a skyline she didn't recognize, and a profusion of flowers overflowing a credenza in a room that wasn't her own.

"Where am I? The last thing I remember was being out in the west pasture with a broken fence to mend, dragging a roll of wire from the bed of a pickup."

"That was three days ago, before you were medevaced to Foothills for treatment. You've been unconscious most of the time since then."

"I remember...some of it." To her absolute horror, her eyes started to burn, her throat felt tight, and her teeth chattered. She gulped in air but couldn't manage a decent breath. Reece advanced and she held up a hand to warn him away. "Back off. I'm f-fine."

"Nice try, but I'm not buying it." Banding her in his familiar strength, her arms fell around his neck as he lifted her higher against the pillows. Settling her there, the pads of his fingers moved to her shoulders and kneaded them in soothing circles. "Lay still."

Phantom pain, it's what she felt with each stroke of his hands. Her mind and body forgot all about her near-death experience while rekindling the intimate connection she had once shared with Reece. *Don't do this. Leave me alone.*

"Okay, I'm good. You've said hello and now, I want you to leave." God, she couldn't look him in the eye, not while he touched her. She pushed his hands aside. "Thanks for stopping by. Maybe we'll see each other again in another decade or two."

"Wimping out on me already?" Reece cupped her chin in his hand and turned her to face him. "I've waited three days for you to regain consciousness, took care of you while I waited. So now, you're going to humor me."

"I beg your damn pardon." She glared at him, her temper mounting. If looks could kill, he would be writhing on the floor at her feet by now. "Who gave you permission to touch me?"

A low, humorless rumble welled up from his chest. "Here's irony for you. Your daddy sent for me to watch over you. It seems someone doesn't like you, although I can't imagine why, given your sunny disposition. Like it or not, peaches—I'm your bodyguard."

BILLIE SLOUCHED IN the taxi, scanning the hospital entrance for Reece while she buckled up. "Take off now! There's an extra fifty in it for you if we aren't followed."

"Sounds like fun." The sedan shot away from the curb with a screech of tires on the asphalt. "Where are we headed?"

Surprised by the throaty voice, Billie looked up to meet a young woman's gaze in the rear-view mirror. Fine lines creased the corners of her mouth. They made her appear older than she was; competent and tough. A face like hers had stories to tell and not all of them pretty. Satisfied she could handle the cab like a pro, Billie gave her directions to the *Circle B*. "It's normally about a two hour drive from here in traffic. How long before you think we can get there?"

"If I get a speeding ticket, you're paying it, right?"

"Absolutely."

"The name's Rena. What's yours?"

"Billie."

Rena tossed her ball cap on the seat, slid sunglasses up her nose, and flexed tattooed knuckles on the steering wheel. *Prison tats. Oh joy.* A nose ring glinted when she turned in her seat to flash a toothy smile. "Whooeee! I've always wanted to do this, although it'd be lots more fun on my Hog. Still, let's see if I can cut the time down by half. Hold on!"

While Rena accelerated with G-force enthusiasm, Billie slammed back in the seat with a grin. Momentary pain throbbed in her head. Still, it was worth it. Reece would look like an idiot when she pulled up at the ranch house without him. Problem solved, her father would throw the bodyguard out on his yummy butt for not doing his job. He thought he could sneak back into her life, did he?

*I think not. Bodyguard my luggage, you jackass.*

She lowered the window a few inches to savor the rush of wind on her face and lack of exhaust fumes in the air after Rena gained the highway. They whizzed past cars at breakneck speed, zooming in and out of sparse traffic. Freedom filled Billie with smug defiance as Rena added to the distance between her and Reece. Some bodyguard he was. While he had checked her out of the hospital, gotten her prescriptions, and the requisite wheelchair to take her out of the building, she'd rode the service elevator down to the ground floor, sailed out the main entrance to the taxi stand, and made a clean getaway. She pumped her fist in the air. *A piece of cake.*

Rena shot a glance over her shoulder and brayed like a mule. "Quite the fashion statement you've got going for yourself. I'm more of a Victoria's Secret gal myself."

"What?" Glancing down, Billie realized she was still wearing her *Save a horse, ride a cowboy* nightshirt and *Rootin' Tootin' Sharp Shootin'* slippers Dottie and Pike had brought to the hospital as a joke to cheer her up. *Oops.*

"I was in kind of a rush when I got out of bed."

"Okey dokey." Rena rolled her eyes, looking in the rear-view. "As long as you're wearing your cowgirl underpants on my upholstery."

Billie gave her the thumbs-up sign while still gloating about her great escape. Reece hadn't had a clue, the big sap. He thought she'd fallen in line with his bodyguard gig, end of story. Typical of the man, thinking he could flex his muscles, curl a finger in her direction, and she would do whatever he wanted like Pavlov's dog. She wasn't a star-struck teen anymore.

Sure, there was a time she would have followed the bull rider to the ends of the earth just to admire his champion belt buckles, not that *she* was a buckle bunny. Heck no. She'd been a celebrity in her own right, a champion barrel racer. They had headlined as 'Rocket' and 'Rocket Girl' in their teenage rodeo days. Actually, Billie still headlined as 'Rocket Girl', since she'd built her reputation under the alias. But, no more Rocket. It was hard to believe she'd only had eyes for him back then—fool that she was.

"Cop alert! There's one gaining on our tail. We gotta stop." Rena eased off the gas pedal, pulled onto the shoulder, and came to a rolling halt. She shoved the transmission into park and leaned back against the headrest, speaking out of the side of her mouth. "Be cool and stay quiet. I know how to handle these guys. As soon as he writes me up a ticket, I'll let him pull out in front and we're away again. There's a shortcut off the next exit ramp that'll work fine for us."

"I'm cool." Judging by her prison artwork, Billie guessed Rena knew a lot of shortcuts to stay off police radar. *It could work.* She swivelled in her seat in time to see a shiny black SUV, with bar lights flashing, nose up behind them.

The door opened. *Uh-oh!* She recognized Reece stepping to the pavement wearing black on black boots, jeans, and a polo shirt. A grin rode his face. Sidling up to Rena's window, he removed his shades, tucked them in his neckband, and squeezed past her ample chest to snatch the keys from the ignition.

"Is there a problem, officer?" Rena gulped, looking guilty enough to have a dead body stashed in her trunk. Maybe she did. Or maybe she liked the feel of Reece's arm brushing her boobs. Billie didn't dare ask.

Reece smirked, his emerald gaze dragging up from Rena's cleavage to her face. "Apparently not, since you're still alive. Your cab fare escaped from the psych ward about a half hour ago. Just so you know; the last cabbie she rode with ended up in a ditch by the side of the road with his throat slashed from ear-to-ear."

"You're shittin' me!" Rena leapt from the car and into Reece's arms, no doubt to avoid the Bowie knife Billie must have stashed in her change purse.

"It's okay, you're safe now." Reece patted her shoulders and stood her off to the side. "You'd better stand back though...just in case."

Springing the back door, he wasted no time lifting Billie across the seat and onto the pavement. The second her cowgirl slippers touched solid ground, she wound up and socked him hard in the mouth. "You lying sack of maggots!"

Reece snapped back from her flailing fists, tugged her wrists behind her back, and slapped on the flex cuffs. Flattening her against the car with his rump, he swiped blood from his split lip and angled his chin at Rena. "See what I mean? The woman's got a hard-on for violence."

"Get out of town. I thought she was weird, but the harmless kind, you know?"

"Trust me. There is nothing harmless about her." He jerked his head in Billie's direction. "Shot up a biker bar once because there weren't any western tunes on the jukebox."

"Hates bikers, does she?" Rena's narrowed gaze said it all. *Traitor*. She'd warmed up to the conversation and almost swooned at Reece's bad boy charms. "Looks like you arrived in the nick of time."

"Don't listen to him, Rena." Billie jumped up and down to get a clear view over Reece's shoulder. "I *love* bikers. He's lying, and he's not a cop!"

The woman rolled her eyes. "Listen, Billie, I know cop cars and that's a fancy unmarked he's driving. Besides, anyone who'd wear the getup you've got on has got to be nuts."

Winking at Reece, Rena retrieved her keys and ambled back to the Chevy, squeezing her chest behind the steering wheel. "Thanks for saving my ass, man."

"Goes with the territory to save a pretty woman," he said. "I'm glad no blood was spilled. Yet."

Snorting in disgust, Billie was jerked to Reece's side as he warned her to shut it with a venomous glare. Opening his wallet, he extracted a crisp hundred dollar bill and pressed it into Rena's palm. "Here's for your trouble. I'll collect it from the jerk who let her escape. From now on, you be careful who crawls into your back seat."

"Oh, I will. It's hard enough to make a living without freaks like her twisting in the breeze." Cranking the key, Rena shot Billie the universal finger, waited for a break in traffic, and peeled rubber for her next cab fare. "Nice doing business with yaaaaaa!"

"THAT WAS A NEW LOW, Reece, even for you." Flex cuffs removed, Billie clambered into the SUV under her own steam. She scrambled across to the passenger's seat and huffed at him when he dropped into the driver's side and started the engine. "How did you find me?"

A trained observer, Reece soaked up the hostility of her body language and made an educated guess. Billie was pissed off, although he wasn't sure if it had more to do with the past than his bodyguard gig. She was madder than a rattlesnake caught in the talons of a hawk—and just about as mean.

"Did you hear what I said? I have a right to know." She kicked a foot at the glove box while flailing an arm at his midsection.

*Oomph.* He sucked in air and rubbed the burn in his stomach. "You have the *right* to keep your hands to yourself, or I'll toss you in the cage. What's it going to be?"

She craned her neck to peer behind them, surveyed the steel mesh enclosure in the back of the SUV, and smirked, dimples riding the corners of her mouth. "You wouldn't dare. That would be too ballsy, even for you."

"Don't push me, peaches. My buddy uses it to transport tracking dogs, but I'll make an exception in your case."

"Bite me."

Oh, he wanted to, and that was the problem. The years hadn't lessened the tightening of his groin when she was within breathing distance. She had grown into herself, her body made for endless nights of lovemaking. Long legs. Rounded hips. Small waist. Full breasts with their little buds peaked slightly upward.

*Don't go there.*

"Knock it off, Billie."

It wasn't just her body. Or the clean scrubbed face Hollywood actresses would hanker after. Or her amazing scent—all things sultry and fresh. It was the total package, the whole enchilada. Throw in the raw passion for living that shone through those smoke-gray eyes and she was a firestorm.

He should have stayed the hell away.

Couldn't...not with her life on the line. But, the quicker he caught the bastard who had hurt her, the faster he could beat boots out of there. This whole thing made him damned uncomfortable, more so because his stupid brain seemed to connect Billie with home—as if he'd ever had a real home.

He hit the bar lights to turn them off and gunned the engine to escape his meandering thoughts. Billie flew back against her seat, grabbing both the armrest and the dash in a death grip while her feet welded to the floor.

"Jeez, Rocket. Speed limits are more than just suggestions, you know? Is there some reason we're hurtling down the highway faster than the speed of light? A reason other than the obvious one, that you want to get us both killed?"

He didn't respond. A sideways glance revealed her game face—as transparent as the panties she wore beneath that ridiculous nightshirt. Yeah, he had ordered himself not to look when she climbed into the passenger seat but had ignored his own advice. One way or another, she would bait and harass him all the way to the ranch.

"Did you hear what I said?" Her hand slipped off the dash on a curve of road and came dangerously close to gelding him. In a lightning-fast move, he diverted her thrust and may have shrieked like a little girl.

"Pardon me?" she said. "I didn't quite catch that."

*Damned woman.* It was clear to him now. By the time they arrived at the *Circle B,* she wanted him screaming his head off and out of control. Then she'd pull the ace out of her sleeve, her bullet wound and surgery, and boo-hoo-hoo to Charley Bradshaw about how he'd mistreated her on the drive. Did she really expect her old man to go ballistic and fire his sorry ass? Well, good luck with that. He'd protect Billie with his life, but he wouldn't put up with another minute of her bull roar.

One hand on the wheel, he dialled Bradshaw's cell phone and waited for him to pick up. "It's Reece."

"What's up? Are you heading home with my daughter?"

"On our way. Question—do you mind if Billie sits in back instead of riding up front with me? I have a bed back there. She'll be comfortable, with the added protection of a steel cage."

"Rocket!" The timbre of Charley's voice abruptly changed. "Are you talking about tossing my little gal into a dog crate?"

"Maybe."

"She giving you trouble?"

"You could say that."

He let out an uproarious laugh. "I don't mind telling you, the fruit didn't fall far from the tree when I sired that little hellion. No sirreee. Put me on speakerphone."

Reece punched the button and flashed Billie an eat-dirt-and-die grin. She glared, looking like she wanted to singe his sorry hide with a branding iron. "Daddy's on the line."

"Great." She tossed her mane of blond-streaked curls, covered the bandage on the side of her head with a flick of her fingers, and stuck her straight little nose in the air. "Dad, I..."

"Now you listen and listen good, darlin'. Reece has my permission to drag you home any way he sees fit, and I don't care if it's strapped to his hood like a hunting trophy. So, behave yourself, ya hear?"

"But he..."

"I'll see you when you get here. Have a good trip." Bradshaw hung up.

Billie sat stone-faced beside Reece, obviously smarting from her father's lack of sympathy. Her silence bothered him a little until the sting of his split lip, bruised stomach, and aching guy parts reminded him of the cheap shots she'd taken at his expense. Still, she had been through a lot, seemed shocky, and trapped somewhere between mutiny and mistrust.

"I wasn't the one who tracked you down from the hospital. Your father did, and only because he loves you."

She stared out the side window as if it held the secrets to the galaxy. "That's a laugh. He didn't show this much interest in me before I was shot." She turned in his direction, her expression curious. "How did he find me?"

"We both had a hunch you'd bolt and run, since you never really reacted to me being your bodyguard." He ran a finger over her delicate wrist and played with her watch strap. "Remember when your dad came to the hospital and gave you this snaffle-bit watch? It does double duty as a tracking device. I followed you on an app from my iPhone when you took off in the taxi."

"Men and their gadgets." She crossed her arms over her chest and blew a wisp of hair out of her eyes. "I might have known."

"Your father worries about you." Reece slowed for the exit to a secondary road and headed across country. The blacktop would take them through Hereford and on to the ranch. "You shouldn't hold it against him, considering someone tried to kill you."

"You're both overreacting," she said, her voice barely a whisper. "Tell me, how much is dear old Dad paying you to humiliate me?"

"Not one red cent. It's true, he sent for me when you were shot, but I wouldn't take the money he offered. I'm here because I want to be; I'm staying until we catch the creep who's after you."

When they reached Forest Valley, the closest mid-sized town, Reece considered taking a short break at the local coffee shop. A glance at Billie dozing beside him and the getup she wore, he opted for the drive-thru window instead. Sipping his coffee, he tucked a bottled water for her in a drink holder, pulled out on Main Street again, and headed east on the highway.

A little farther out and the local butcher shop triggered a painful memory; he was twelve-years-old and helping his drunken old man haul a deer carcass to the back door for dressing and packaging. His father had later traded the meat for a couple cases of cheap whiskey. Reece had snared a few rabbits that winter, but game had been scarce. So was food on the table, especially after his mother headed south with a passing trucker. She never returned, not that he blamed her. Life as Dad's punching bag had killed the marriage.

He was seventeen when he'd found his old man crushed beneath the wheels of a tractor. The sheriff said he'd been drunk, fallen out, and run over himself. By this time, his father's death had added more weight to the load, and Reece had built a chip on his shoulder a country-mile wide. When Charley Bradshaw heard the news, he brought him to the *Circle B* to live, and Reece had repaid him by being a mean-tempered jerk. Hell, he'd betrayed everyone's trust...especially Billie's.

He understood now that Charley had done his best to help him grow into a man. In those days, Reece figured he'd topped the chart of native sons most likely to end up in jail, or worse. Hell, he owed the man big time. The least he could do now was keep Billie safe. And keep his hands off her.

Plastic-wrapped round bales of hay sat in the fields skirting the highway. The new mown scent haunted him with memories of driving the baler on the ranch. Lunch breaks in the shade of an old maple tree, the taste of thick ham sandwiches with mustard, and sweet-tart lemonade Billie rode out to him on horseback.

Their stolen kisses had led him to take advantage of her trusting vulnerability. Small wonder she hated his guts now—after the pregnancy he'd caused and the miscarriage she'd suffered without him. He needed to talk to her about those things, but now wasn't the time, not until she was one hundred percent healed. She had enough to deal with, without him dredging up painful memories.

He turned onto a gravel road that intersected the entrance to the ranch, hooked a left, and pulled to a stop at the top of the drive. The old homestead looked the same. He guessed it hadn't changed much in over a hundred years or more. She was a proud old gal, chinked log walls faded to gray. Overhanging porches skirted the main house along three sides, a slanted tin roof reflecting the sun's rays in hues of blue that matched the flowerbeds below. Treed windbreaks and wide open spaces surrounded the ranch house and outbuildings as far as the distant mountains.

Horses gathered in the pasture to his right, their whinnies a familiar and welcoming sound. Reece lowered the windows. They broke into a gallop as soon as he touched the gas pedal, easily beating the SUV down the long drive to the house. He chuckled, imagining they smelled Billie curled up beside him on the passenger seat. They were welcoming her home.

Nudging her awake, he watched her stretch like a cat, push open the door, and drop to the ground, her feet flying toward the gate and her beloved horses the instant she laid eyes on them. Panic gripped him. He grabbed the assault rifle from behind the seat and moved to surround her with his bulk as she passed through the fence.

A sparkle in the distance caught his gaze in an instant. Zeroing in on it with the rifle scope, he scanned the terrain for another flash of light. Uneasiness gripped him. Ten seconds. Twenty seconds. Nothing. Still, someone was out there.

*Does the bastard want another shot at Billie?*

www.ingramcontent.com/pod-product-compliance
Lightning Source LLC
Chambersburg PA
CBHW022108170626
46808CB00002B/655